SHOWCASE

Special Books by Special Writers

The Book:

NOT WITHOUT MY CHILD

A very contemporary and deeply emotional story of love, family…and second chances. You won't be able to put it down!

The Writer:

Rebecca Winters is the award-winning author of *The Wrong Twin*. She's won both the National Readers' Choice Award and the *Romantic Times* Reviewer's Choice Award. She's appeared on bestseller lists and was named the 1995 Utah Writer of the Year.

"Rebecca Winters is a master storyteller whose characters touch your heart. She delivers the ultimate fantasy and captures every woman's dream. A Rebecca Winters romance transports the reader to a magical place, and it's a journey I never want to miss."   —Bonnie K. Winn

"Rebecca Winters is a sterling storyteller whose heroes and heroines make you believe all the warm, wonderful things love can be."   —Betina Lindsey

Rebecca Winters writes "powerful, moving" stories— stories "filled with passion, betrayal and a love so strong as to overcome all obstacles."   —*Affaire de Coeur*

Dear Reader,

It has been said that divorce has no dignity, and therefore it is even more traumatic to the human soul than the death of a spouse.

I wrote this novel, *Not Without My Child*, so you and I could walk in Tessa's footsteps for a few hours and consider the meaning of dignity, explore the *possibility* of dignity.

I think of Tessa as a remarkable woman. She went through a Gethsemane that should have destroyed her. Instead, it refined her and made her strong. When she emerged victorious, she was ready to claim the love of the steadfast man who believed in her, a man worthy of her goodness, courage and faith.

This book is lovingly dedicated to every woman who has ever walked through the shadows.

Rebecca Winters

Rebecca Winters

NOT WITHOUT MY CHILD

Harlequin Books

TORONTO • NEW YORK • LONDON
AMSTERDAM • PARIS • SYDNEY • HAMBURG
STOCKHOLM • ATHENS • TOKYO • MILAN
MADRID • WARSAW • BUDAPEST • AUCKLAND

ISBN 0-373-70697-9

NOT WITHOUT MY CHILD

NOT WITHOUT MY CHILD

CHAPTER ONE

"...SO I'VE DECIDED not to wait any longer. I'm asking Grant for a divorce."

The man sitting in the swivel chair behind the desk said nothing, only continued to listen with his fingertips pressed together beneath his chin.

Tess Marsden had learned not to expect any support from her psychiatrist regarding problems in her marriage, but it no longer mattered. She was going to divorce Grant.

"Since you know him well, Dr. Milhouse, I wondered if you had any advice on how I should tell him. It won't come as a surprise to him, though. He's never actually said the word 'divorce,' but I'm sure he's as anxious as I am to end the pain."

"And you've come to this conclusion since your trip to Hawaii?"

Tess schooled herself not to react, but everything about Dr. Milhouse repulsed her. She'd been his patient for more than four years. He knew her six-year marriage had been a disaster from the start. How could he have asked her such a ridiculous question?

If her own father hadn't referred her to Dr. Milhouse on the strength of a colleague's recommendation, Tess would never have kept her second appointment with him.

To her horror, instead of helping her overcome a short-term postpartum depression, he'd diagnosed her with bipolar disorder, which meant she was manic-depressive. Her mood swings, he'd said, would have to be controlled by medication for the rest of her life.

The dosage was given according to the results of twice-monthly blood tests, which he monitored closely, then followed up with office visits.

She'd dreaded every moment spent in his office. Right from the start he'd attempted to control her life, even her feelings. As a result, she'd closed up long ago, rarely revealing anything of a personal nature. But she had hoped for a little advice before confronting Grant, since the doctor knew her husband well.

Choosing her words carefully, she said, "If it wasn't for my religious convictions, I probably would have divorced him before Scotty was born. It took me some time to realize I didn't fit the image Grant had of me. He thought he was marrying a Michelle Pfeiffer and enjoyed showing me off to business contacts. It was like I was on display all the time."

She took a breath and went on, "He wouldn't let me be just a 'normal' housewife. The more he tried to change me, the more estranged we became. This last year has been impossible, and I've finally admitted to myself that I can't go on this way."

Dr. Milhouse, she noticed, didn't so much as raise a brow. "To my surprise," she said, "when I told my brother, Winn, what I was thinking of doing, he said, 'Hallelujah,' and begged me to go to Hawaii with him and Rae and the kids so we could talk everything out first.

"I told Grant about my going with them and taking Scotty with me. Winn said he'd pay for everything."

Tess sighed. "At first Grant seemed resentful. Probably because we've never been able to afford to go anyplace special for a vacation. But when I reminded him that the tension had been unbearable, he admitted it might be a good idea. So Scotty and I went."

"How long were you gone?"

"Eight days."

"Your trip obviously agreed with you."

"It did. I'm glad I went. Scotty and I haven't had that much fun in years. It was wonderful to put some distance between me and Grant. I gained a whole new perspective."

"Did you meet a man?"

The blandly stated question infuriated her.

"Why would you ask me that?"

"I can see I hit a nerve. You'd be surprised how many of my patients come back from vacations with a whole new lease on life. It generally means they've met someone outside their normal range of experience and they can disconnect themselves from their problems for a little while. It's entirely normal."

Actually she *had* met a man who wasn't made from the same mold as the people she knew. The experience had been illuminating and had defined certain things for her. But she hadn't had an affair, if that was what the doctor meant, and she was quite certain he did. She suspected he would enjoy hearing all the details.

Tess stared at him in loathing. His total lack of insight and sensitivity at such a crucial moment in her life took away any residual guilt she'd been harboring over what she was about to do.

"Let's just say the trip reaffirmed my need for a divorce." She leaned forward. "So, can you suggest any tactful way I might put this to Grant? I don't want to hurt him."

The doctor pursed his lips. "Look. Promise me you won't say or do anything until I've had a chance to talk to him. Then I want to see you again in two weeks. Be sure and bring a urine sample with you."

"All right," she said, though she had no intention of keeping her next appointment. If everything worked out the way she prayed it would, she would never have to see a psychiatrist again. But no matter the outcome, she would never go back to Dr. Milhouse. The thought filled her with so much elation she feared it showed. "Shall I tell Grant you want to see him?"

"No. I'll call him directly."

"Thank you, Doctor."

"No problem." Then he reached for his prescription pad. He wrote out the order to renew her medication and handed it to her. "Tess?"

"Yes?" She'd gotten to her feet, on the verge of leaving.

"You sound happier than I've heard you in years."

She had the distinct feeling he wasn't at all pleased by that. "I am. And you know why? Because the pain doesn't have to go on and on. Grant is a good person. I can still say that about him, but I'd like to get out of our marriage before I reach the point where I can't. Understand?"

Dr. Milhouse nodded. "As soon as I've talked with Grant, I'll call you to come in again."

DR. MILHOUSE buzzed his nurse and told her to give him five minutes before she sent in his next patient. Then he reached for Tessa Marsden's file. He pulled a pen from the pocket of his lab coat and wrote:

January 20—Patient has returned from trip and is preoccupied with ideas of divorcing her husband. I don't like her euphoria, which is much more pronounced than it was four years ago when she first talked of divorce.

I'll inform her husband that her evasiveness suggests a possible liaison with a man she met in Hawaii. She should never have been allowed to go on that trip. Suspect she was introduced to illicit drugs and needs constant supervision.

Would have checked her urine this visit, but she is showing classic signs of resisting me and keeping secrets. Will do a pregnancy check, as well as tests for possible traces of cocaine, speed or amphetamines in urine on next visit February 3.

Have increased her Valium to 2.5 mg po quid prn anxiety and lithium carbonate to 300 mg po tid. If that doesn't slow her down, then stronger measures will have to be taken. Will advise husband to keep her under strict surveillance.

FOR THE FIRST TIME in four years Tess didn't stop at the pharmacy on her way out. The feeling was so liberating she practically danced to her car.

It was almost eleven. Her father would have finished his hospital rounds and be at his office by now. She hoped he'd be able to fit her in between patients.

Five minutes later she pulled into the parking lot of the Colorado Springs Clinic of Orthopedic Surgery. As always, the reception room was packed, but the friendly woman at the front desk told her to go on back; her father'd be thrilled to see her.

Though Richard Jenner was in his late sixties, he still had a full head of hair, the same rich dark brown as Tess's. A tall man, temperate in every way, he wore the size-forty-two suit he'd always worn. He had a smile for everyone, and his patients adored him. So did Tess.

"Hi, Daddy."

"Honey, you're back! I wondered when I was going to hear from you. Winn phoned early this morning."

"I hope you don't mind my interrupting like this." She went around his desk where he was working on his charts and hugged him.

"Shame on you for saying that." He looked at her with pride. "I don't need to ask if you had a good time. You're so tanned, and beautiful as always."

"Thanks, Daddy. Hawaii was wonderful. I'll never be able to thank Rae and Winn enough for asking me and Scotty along."

"Everyone needs to get away once in a while."

She hugged him again. Her father was the most tactful diplomatic man she'd ever known. It was his way of saying he knew she was unhappy in her marriage, but he'd never pry.

She swallowed hard, keeping her hand on his shoulder. "Daddy...do you have a few minutes to talk?"

He must have sensed her anxiety because he said, "I'll make time." He spoke into the intercom, asking his nurse not to disturb them.

Tess walked over and shut the door before sitting down on a chair near his desk.

"I met a man in Hawaii named Paul Wong, the owner of the hotel where we were staying. To get to the point, he had a son who drowned in the ocean when he was Scotty's age. For some reason, Scotty reminded him of his son, and he doted on him while we were there. We all became good friends.''

Her father nodded. ''Winn told me.''

''Well, I guess during one of their conversations, Scotty told him I had to take medication every day to survive. Paul doesn't believe in Western medicine. In a very polite way, he asked me why I was on the drugs.''

''What did you tell him?''

''I explained what happened to me after Scotty was born.'' She paused and studied her father's solemn expression before going on. ''I told him how I was diagnosed with bipolar disorder, and how much I hated taking the medicine. It makes me feel slow and dull-witted, like I'm wrapped in cotton swabbing.''

She smiled. ''Paul was such a wonderful listener I found myself telling him other things, as well. Things I've wanted to confide in you, but I haven't dared because . . . you were the one who referred me to Dr. Milhouse in the first place.''

A rare frown creased her father's brow. ''Honey, you can tell me anything. What are you getting at?''

''I—I've never liked Dr. Milhouse. And I've come to realize he enjoyed controlling me with drugs. He wasn't any real help to me beyond dispensing my medication. When I told Paul about him, he agreed with me that Dr. Milhouse has been manipulative, leaving me with no sense of hope about my condition or my marriage, thereby making me more and more dependent on medicine.''

She took a deep breath. "Paul has challenged me to stop taking the drugs and see what happens.''

"Thank God!''

Her father's reaction was so unexpected she was shocked. "Then you don't think I'm crazy?''

He shook his head. "On the contrary, I think you're the bravest person I know. I'm indebted to this man for suggesting something that I should've discussed with you. *Intended* to discuss with you.''

"You did? But why...?''

"Honey, I was devastated when Dr. Milhouse diagnosed you as manic-depressive. I knew it meant constant medication. I always felt he moved too soon on that diagnosis. But since I'm the one who told you to go and see him on the advice of a trusted colleague, I couldn't very well argue with his treatment.''

He sighed. "I didn't say anything to you because I knew how precarious things were with you and Grant. I didn't want him to see it as interference. But your mother and I aren't blind to your marital difficulties and realize you can't go on this way much longer. That's the reason Winn invited you to go to Hawaii.''

Tess hadn't confided in her parents because she hadn't wanted to burden them, yet they'd known all along! She felt warmth flood her.

"I'm so glad!" she cried. "I want to stop cold turkey, the way Uncle Jess quit smoking. As Paul said, the worst that can happen is that I go back into depression like I did after I had Scotty. If that's the case, I'll consult another psychiatrist and go from there. But if Paul's right and I don't need medicine—if my condition has reversed itself—then I've got to find that out, too. I'd like to do it before I ask Grant for a divorce."

"I'm with you all the way, honey."

Encouraged, she said, "Paul's reasoning makes perfect sense. After all, I'd never suffered depression until after my baby was born. He thinks I was depressed over my marriage."

"With good reason," her father concurred. "Your mother and I have often speculated that if you had divorced Grant before Scotty was born, you might never have suffered any depression at all."

"Oh, Daddy, I'm so grateful you support me in this. I have to find out one way or the other, before I file."

"Honey, I'd give anything on earth to see you happy again. I'll do whatever it takes to make that possible."

"Thank you. That means everything to me," she whispered, and threw her arms around his neck. They hugged for a long time.

When at last they pulled apart, Tess gazed at her father, her eyes shiny with tears, and said, "Do you know that since I was diagnosed, Grant has treated me like a handicapped child? It's such an irony. He says he doesn't believe in psychiatry, yet he's good friends with Dr. Milhouse and watches over me to make sure I keep every appointment and take my medication. Things between us have degenerated so much we haven't been intimate in I don't know how long."

Her father grimaced. "In a marriage, illness of any kind is difficult to deal with. Grant should have been more understanding and supportive. Unfortunately it would take a mature man to understand your problem and not be frightened by it. I'm afraid maturity is not one of your husband's strong suits."

"No," she agreed. Again her father's frankness surprised her. Normally he was careful not to criticize. "Daddy? What are the dangers of cutting off the drugs?"

"You won't notice any effect from the lithium. But you've been on Valium for close to four years. To go off it means you'll suffer anxiety, panic attacks. I'd like to hospitalize you for the first forty-eight hours to monitor your heart."

Tess didn't care what the risks were. "All right, whatever you think is best." A pause, then, "How can we keep this from Dr. Milhouse? He and Grant are the last two people I want to know anything. Every time I told Grant I'd like to stop taking the medicine, he erupted. Dr. Milhouse has Grant convinced he knows what's best for me."

"Under the circumstances, I agree this should be our family secret." Her father rubbed his chin thoughtfully. "I have a solution. We can plan a family ski trip to the cabin. Grant's never been able to get away during the week, so he probably wouldn't join us till the weekend." He glanced over at Tess, who nodded.

"You can take Scotty out of school," he went on. "While your mother deals with him, I'll admit you to the hospital in Vail—I have privileges there. After two days we'll go back to the cabin until the weekend for lots of walks, fresh air, relaxing evenings in front of the fire."

He gazed lovingly at his daughter. "Your withdrawal won't take as long as some because you've never used stimulants. In a few weeks you should be completely and safely through it. By that time we'll have a fairly good idea of your physical and mental state."

"You'd do that for me, Daddy?"

"I'd do anything to have my happy darling Tess back."

"I'll never be able to thank you enough." Her voice trembled.

"Nonsense. Now, let's not waste any time. The fellows owe me. I only have two operations scheduled for this week, and both can be rescheduled. We can leave for Vail tonight. That'll give us Tuesday through Friday. If Grant joins us, he won't come before Friday night or Saturday, right? By that time you'll have been through the worst."

"So does that mean I can forget taking any medicine today?"

He reached for her hand and squeezed it. "That's exactly what it means. You go on home and tell your mother our plans. I'll call the hospital in Vail and arrange for your admission tonight. What are you going to say to Grant?"

She'd been worrying about that herself. "I'll tell him that since you have some time off, I'm anxious to spend a little time with you and Mom. I don't think he'll suspect anything. I pray he won't."

"I doubt it would occur to him you'd be brave enough to try such an experiment. What he's forgotten, though, is you're a Jenner, and Jenners have hidden reserves of strength. They pull them out when they're needed."

"Speak for yourself." She smiled. "I couldn't even think of doing this without you."

"You've got me, honey. You've always had me and you always will. Don't ever forget it."

"I won't. Now I'd better hurry home so I can phone Grant and set things up."

"Come here first and give your old dad one more hug before you go."

"MR. MARSDEN? Your wife is on line one."

My wife. What a joke. "Thanks, Cindy."

Grant glared at the blinking light. A wife was supposed to be synonymous with great sex whenever you wanted it. That was what marriage was all about.

Not only had sex never been great with Tessa, it was now nonexistent, and he'd been stuck with the booby prize.

The day of their wedding, he'd congratulated himself on marrying the most beautiful girl on campus. Every guy in his fraternity envied him for snagging the Sweetheart of Theta Chi.

They'd laugh their heads off if they knew what a disappointment she'd turned out to be. The goddess exterior didn't match the inhibited frigid bride who'd ruined his honeymoon, become a boring housewife and turned psycho on him after Scotty was born.

Damn you, Tess, for cheating me out of the best years of my life!

And, except that she looked more beautiful than usual with a tan, nothing had changed since her arrival home from Hawaii the day before yesterday.

Not that he'd expected any miracles. Years ago Dr. Milhouse had disabused him on that score. Tessa would be a mental case for the rest of her life, and there wasn't one damn thing Grant could do about it.

On the surface she pretended everything was normal. She fixed his meals, kept a clean house, answered his questions and maintained a polite civility in front of Scotty—but they hadn't had sex in months. Now, for some reason, she was calling him at the office. Nothing short of an emergency would have roused her from her stupor to do that.

He punched the button. "What's going on, Tessa?" He wondered if she was calling from the psychiatrist's office.

"I'm sorry to bother you when you're working, but I wanted to ask if it would be all right if I went up to the cabin for the rest of the week with Mom and Dad. I haven't spent any time with them in months."

"Did I say you hadn't?" he retorted.

"No." Her tone was calm, collected. It was the tone he despised. "I didn't mean to imply that, Grant. But since I've only just returned from Hawaii, I was afraid you might mind my being gone again so soon."

"And if I do mind?"

There was a slight pause. "If you don't want me to go, I won't."

If she'd been capable of fulfilling even one of his fantasies, he'd be home like a shot and she wouldn't be going anywhere. But there wasn't a hope in hell of that happening.

"No. Go, but what about Scotty?"

"Naturally I'll take him with me. Except for the trip to Hawaii, he hasn't missed any school this year. A few more days won't hurt. Grant... just so you know, I've made a couple of casseroles and put them in the freezer for you."

A casserole. The very thing he wanted after a hard day's work. "Am I supposed to thank you for that?"

"Please, let's not quarrel. We're leaving this afternoon. Scotty and I will be home Sunday evening."

"I'm overjoyed."

In a foul mood, he hung up the receiver, only to be buzzed by his secretary again. Dr. Milhouse's nurse was on the phone for a second time, wanting to set up an appointment with him. Said it was urgent.

Now what, he wondered, was so important that it couldn't wait a couple of days? He was supposed to be seeing Howard Milhouse later in the week....

HOWARD STOOD UP from his desk to greet Grant Marsden. Not for the first time he was reminded of a younger Dabney Coleman, mustache and all. Today Grant was immaculately dressed in a dark green blazer and tan khakis, not a hair out of place.

"Have a seat, Grant," he said after they shook hands.

"Thanks. What's going on? Your nurse said it was urgent. Don't tell me Tessa's worse."

Howard cocked his head. "Have you noticed anything different about her this time?"

"You mean since the trip?"

"Since the trip or since my last visit with you a month ago."

"No." He laughed, but without humor. "She's still a zombie."

"She *has* to take the drugs I've prescribed, Grant. It's not a choice."

"Whatever. All I know is, I don't have a sex life. I just go to work, come home late, eat dinner and go to bed." His hazel eyes shifted to Howard. "Why are you asking me if I've noticed anything?"

"Because I saw a distinct change in her this morning."

Grant leaned forward, his hands clasped between his knees. "What kind of change?"

"She's more excited, more manic. I was hoping you might know why."

Grant hunched his shoulders and shook his head. "What are you getting at, exactly?"

"I have reason to believe your wife might be taking drugs."

Grant's head jerked up. "You mean, on top of what you give her? Cocaine or something? Tessa?"

"Cocaine...or speed. I don't have proof yet. I'll test her urine on the next visit and it'll tell me what I want to know. But all the signs are there."

"Like what?"

"As I said, an excitement, a new energy. I had to increase the strength of her Valium."

"Great," came the bitter rejoinder.

Howard let the comment pass. "Does her brother ever do drugs, Grant? Or your sister-in-law?"

"Not that I know of. I think I'd have noticed by now. Her brother's a successful architect and they could certainly afford to indulge in recreational drugs, but it would be a new one on me. They're high society in Colorado Springs, do a lot of entertaining..."

"Do *you* do drugs, Grant?"

"I used to a bit when I was in college."

"So you don't have them around the house."

"No. If I wanted to do them, I'd call a couple of old fraternity brothers."

"Then we have to conclude she did them while she was in Hawaii." By the look on Grant's face, the thought had never occurred to him. "I've warned you before to keep closer tabs on your wife because of her illness. She probably met a man who introduced her to them."

"Hell." Grant stared hard at Howard. "I have a feeling you're on to something. Just this morning Tessa called to tell me she's leaving again to spend the rest of the week at the cabin near Vail with her parents. She's already left, in fact."

Howard nodded. "That would explain her euphoria in my office. Are you sure she went to the cabin? Do you know for a fact that her parents will be there with her?"

"No, but I can find out with one phone call to Dr. Jenner's office." His eyes narrowed. "If Tessa did meet someone who got her hooked on drugs, then she's hit rock bottom. I tell you, that's it!"

"I understand how you feel. You're her husband. If you could get the proof, you could have her institutionalized."

Grant squinted at Howard. "You mean have her locked up?"

"It would be for her own good. Taking cocaine or amphetamines on top of her prescribed medication could kill her. But if she was in a controlled environment, she'd be safe, and you could visit her on a regular basis, yet still be free to live your own life. Of course you'd have to catch her in the act."

Howard could see the wheels turning. "I could drive up there and surprise her," Grant said. "I've got a couple of appointments tonight and tomorrow night, but I could go after that."

"You could, but you'd need a plan. Tell me—how long has it been since you've had...relations with your wife?"

"I don't know. Seven, eight months maybe."

"So, you take her roses. Tell her you've planned a romantic evening as a sort of welcome-home-from-Hawaii celebration. Sometimes the unexpected acts as an aphrodisiac."

"My wife's dead from the forehead down," Grant muttered, his bitterness more pronounced.

"Even if that's true, if you went to the cabin—assuming she's there—it would serve two purposes. One, it would show her you're still trying to be a loving husband. Two, you would discover if she's doing drugs. Naturally I'm concerned for her health." When the younger man didn't say anything, Howard asked, "Do you still desire your wife, Grant?"

There was a long pause. "She's the best-looking woman I've ever seen, but she's never met one of my expectations. Our honeymoon was a joke."

"You mean she's not responsive sexually."

"You could put it that way."

"Has she ever refused you?"

"No. Let's just say she never got into it, which is the worst turn off of all. I always believed a man had the right to have fun and fool around with his wife whenever he felt like it. Tessa's been a pain from day one.

"After we got married, she refused to dress in the kind of clothes I picked out for her. She's a knock-out and ought to show herself off more, but she prefers a sort of demure, tailored look."

He snorted in disgust. "In the insurance business, I have to rely on a lot of socializing, evening engagements to build a clientele. Tessa could be the perfect asset for that kind of thing. Men swarm around her, making it twice as easy for me to pick up new contacts and referrals."

A grimace marred his good-looking features. "But wouldn't you know it? She hates socializing, and as soon as she got pregnant, she used every excuse to stay home. And then once Scotty was born, she doted on him and turned into a real wimp. Thanks to her, the past six years have been hell, and my business hasn't grown all that much."

"Well, you know what you can do about it, Grant. If you don't want to miss out on any more, then the first step is to discover your wife's whereabouts and see if she's into drugs. Call me when you have any news. Otherwise I'll talk to you after your wife's next appointment.''

The two men shook hands. As soon as Grant left, Howard checked his watch. If he didn't hurry, he was going to be late for his latest hospital admission.

He found Tessa Marsden's file and quickly added more notes to the ones he'd written earlier in the day:

Patient's husband in for visit at my request. I've informed him of my fear his wife's taking amphetamines. Have suggested a technique to uncover the truth. Have suggested possibility of institutionalizing the patient for her own safety. Husband will keep me posted. It may be necessary to wait until patient's next appointment to ascertain the truth.

CHAPTER TWO

"DR. JENNER?" One of the emergency-room attendants popped his head around the curtain. "Your wife's on line two. She says it's important. You can talk on the wall phone outside the cubicle."

"Thanks, Arney."

He wiped the moisture from Tess's face with a tissue. His brave beautiful daughter was in agony, and there wasn't anything he could do about it. After forty hours of watching her climb the walls with agitation and anxiety attacks, he was also aware that she'd begun having chest pains.

He was terrified she might have a heart attack, but Tess remained adamant about freeing herself from the bondage of medication. She was willing to put up with anything, even the risk of death. How he admired her! She was so strong, so courageous.

"Honey," he said to her, "it's your mom on the phone. I'll be right back."

"Hurry, Daddy," Tess implored, her jaws clenched and features tautened against the pain.

Richard pulled his hand from hers and dashed out of the cubicle.

He picked up the receiver, pressing the line-two button. "Wilma?"

"How is she?"

"She's having some chest pain, but if it doesn't get any worse, she should be able to leave here in a few hours."

"Oh, Richard." Wilma started to sob. "Maybe we shouldn't have let her do this."

"She didn't give us a choice."

"She's so brave. Much braver than I could've been."

"Tess is remarkable. All we can do is pray, sweetheart."

The line was silent for a moment, then Wilma said, "I've got some bad news." Her voice shook.

"Grant?"

"Yes. Would you believe he showed up at the cabin a little while ago?"

Richard shook his head. "Oh, no."

"It's almost like he knew."

"What did you tell him?"

"That you and Tess accepted an invitation from old family friends to ski with them and have dinner after. I told him I didn't expect you home until quite late. He's not at all happy about it."

Perspiration beaded Richard's brow. "Where is he now?"

"Building a snowman with Scotty. But it's getting dark out, so they'll probably be in any minute."

"Pacify him as long as you can. I can't leave Tess."

"I wouldn't want you to. And, Richard, if she gets any worse, call me. I don't care if Grant finds out. We all need to be there for her."

"I agree, sweetheart."

He hung up and hurried back into the cubicle. Miraculously she looked a little more relaxed. "Honey?"

"It's passing. The pain is passing."

"Thank God," he whispered, knowing it could come back at any time. He bent over and kissed her clammy forehead. The hair around her face lay in damp tendrils. Thirty-eight years of practice had not dulled Richard's compassion for human suffering. To see his own daughter suffer was almost more than he could bear. "Your mother sends her love."

"Is everything all right? Scotty?"

"He's fine."

"Daddy? Do you think the pain will come back?"

"No," he said, praying it was the truth. "I don't. I think you're through the worst of this, my darling." He grabbed her hand and held it tight.

His prayers were answered, because by ten that night there'd been no recurrence of the pain and the wires to the heart monitor were unhooked so she could get up. Richard reached out to help her.

"No," she said. "I can do this on my own." After several unsteady attempts, she made it to the door of the bathroom. Again he marveled at her strength and determination.

When she reappeared she said, "Can we go home now? I'm feeling okay."

"Sure?"

She nodded.

"All right. While you get dressed, I'll go out and sign your release papers."

"Daddy?" Her eyes filled. "How can I ever thank you?"

He pulled her into his arms and held her while she wept. "Do you know how lucky I am to have a daughter like you?"

"How can you say that when I've been such a worry ever since Scotty was born?"

He cringed. "Oh, honey, have I done something to make you feel that way?"

"Nothing. It's just me."

He smoothed the hair from her temples and made her look at him. "Honey, you can't help what's happened, or the way things are going between you and Grant. I'm going to confess something I shouldn't, but I think it's important for you to know.

"In my opinion—and your mother shares it—Grant isn't the most . . . lovable of men. He seems to be angry at the world, probably a carryover from his childhood. You have nothing to do with his problem."

"Well, all it proves is that I'm the world's worst judge of character, because I didn't see it while we were dating."

"Don't you know all young people are blind when their hormones are raging?" He winked at her. "All it proves is that you haven't met the right man yet. We have to play the cards that are dealt to us. But there're a lot more in the pack—the ace can turn up at any time."

She shook her head and pulled away from him. "Maybe the man for me *is* out there somewhere. Maybe I'll even meet him one day. But if we find out my manic-depression is permanent, he'll say no thanks and pass me by."

"What nonsense. No man in his right mind would ever pass you by."

"Oh, Daddy..." She gave him a reluctant smile, then said, "Well, I guess some women are just luckier. Look at Rae..."

Richard thought of his daughter-in-law. "Yes, but it's because her looks didn't blind Winn to the real person beneath. Sweetheart, you have the kind of beauty most men only fantasize about, but Grant never knew how to see inside."

"You talk as if I'm some kind of femme fatale."

Richard stared at his daughter, who despite her exhausted features and lank hair, was truly lovely. *She really doesn't know.* Her humility touched his heart.

"Okay, let me put it this way. You're a dead ringer for your mother, and she was a real traffic-stopper in her day. Still is, in my book."

That comment brought a wide smile. "She was the luckiest woman in the world to meet you."

"We both were, and one day, you will be, too."

Suddenly her face paled and perspiration broke out along her hairline. "Are you in pain?" he asked in alarm.

"No. I think I'm going to be sick."

Richard helped her into the bathroom, then held a cool cloth to her neck as she vomited. He knew the nausea was to be expected, but his heart went out to her anew.

"Better?" he asked after a moment.

She looked at him and nodded gratefully. "I feel better now. I'll get dressed."

Richard went to the front desk to discharge her. Ten minutes later they were out in the parking lot. They walked around for a few minutes until Tess's nausea had subsided completely. Then he ushered her into the car and soon they were on their way to the cabin.

He glanced over at her. "Honey? There's something you need to know. Scotty's fine," he said quickly when he saw the panic in her eyes. "I waited until now because I didn't want to upset you. Grant's at the cabin."

"You're kidding!"

"No. For some reason he decided to drive up after work. I've been thinking of what excuse we could give him for being this late. Maybe say you've got food poisoning and weren't up to the drive back to the cabin until now."

"That's exactly how it feels."

"The symptoms mask what's really going on. But if you don't think you can handle seeing him right now, we can stay in Vail and think of something else to tell him."

He saw her clench her hands. "No. It's better to face him. I'm going to be sick on and off for the next couple of weeks, right? So in a few days, when I'm not better, we can tell him I've come down with the flu. It's going around, anyway."

Richard nodded. "Good plan."

"What'll I do when it's time to go in for my blood test?"

"I'll call Dr. Milhouse and tell him you're under the weather. That you'll be in as soon as you're better. By four weeks' time we'll have a pretty good idea about your true condition."

She nodded and grasped her father's outstretched hand, squeezing it hard.

AT FOUR IN THE MORNING, Tess rushed to the bathroom and threw up again. When she was through wretching, she clutched the sink and stood trembling until the worst of the nausea had passed.

Grant appeared in the doorway. "What's made you so sick?" Although he'd been sleeping on the couch in the front room, he must have heard her.

"I'm not sure, but I'm sorry to have wakened you. I'm sorry about everything. I know you drove all this way so we could talk."

They hadn't talked earlier when she and her father had arrived. Richard had told Grant that she'd been sick and needed to go straight to bed. Grant hadn't seemed at all pleased by this news, but he'd had no choice but to accept it. She'd been aware that he'd brought her roses, which was totally unexpected; he hadn't brought her flowers since before their marriage.

When he didn't say anything now, she turned to him, surprised to discover his eyes were filled with accusation.

"I really am sorry, Grant." She meant it. Sorry for the trouble in their marriage, sorry that her mere presence provoked such hostility in him.

"*Are* you?"

Another tremor racked her body, but this one had more to do with panic than the withdrawal symptoms. "Please don't start a quarrel. Mom and Dad and Scotty will be able to hear us, and I'm too weak."

"Where did you get the stuff, Tess?"

"Pardon me?"

"You know."

"You're not making any sense."

Disconcerted by his question, she tried to leave the bathroom and go back to bed, but he blocked the way. Another panic attack was coming on. Her heart started pounding like a herd of buffalo thundering across the prairie.

"I once told you that I experimented with drugs in college," he said. "All my friends did, and I can rec-

ognize when a person is coming down off something. So tell me, where have you been getting
drugs?''

"Drugs?'' Her mouth felt like cotton and her skin
was starting to crawl.

"You know what I mean.'' He seemed to enjoy
trapping her there in the bathroom. It frightened her.
"I'm your husband, and I know when you're hiding
something from me.''

"Grant...I don't know what you're talking about.''

"Cut the act, Tess. Are you on cocaine?''

"No! Never!'' Her breath was coming in pants.
"I—I need to lie down.''

He folded his arms, still blocking her way. "Not
until you tell me when you started taking drugs on top
of your medication.''

The buzzing in her ears was getting worse. *Did he
really just ask me if I was taking cocaine?* The bitter
irony made her want to laugh hysterically.

"Did you get it in Hawaii? Answer me, dammit!''

"I—I can't. I'm going to be sick again.'' She turned
to the toilet just in time.

"If you're not going to help your wife, then clear
the doorway so I can.''

Tess heard her father's stern voice somewhere in the
periphery while she vomited.

"Can't you see how sick she is, Grant? I know you
two have serious problems, but your indifference
shouts loud and clear. Some people would call it
abuse.''

"No one's abusing her. She's already done that to herself. Look at her! Who knows what she's been putting in her body that we're not aware of. You're a doctor. You more than anybody ought to be concerned about—"

"I'm very concerned, but now is not the time for discussion. She needs care. If you can't supply that, then go back to Colorado Springs and allow Wilma and me to get her on her feet again."

"That's fine with me. Just so you know, Scotty's leaving with me before he finds out his mother is a drug addict!"

"No!" Tess cried, turning from the toilet. "D-don't wake him!"

"Forget about taking Scotty anywhere," she heard her father say in a withering tone that stunned even Tess. "Getting him up in the middle of the night because you're upset is the worst thing you could do. Right now you're in no state to be with anyone, particularly Scotty. Go home and cool off."

Maybe it was because her father had never spoken to Grant that way before. Whatever it was, her husband left the bathroom without further argument.

A second later, she heard, "Tess?"

"Mom?" Tess reached for her mother and clung to her.

"Come on, darling. Let's get you back to the bedroom."

"Has he gone?"

"Your father's walking him out to the car."

"He didn't take Scotty, did he?"

"No, darling." They'd reached Tess's bed, and Wilma helped her into it. "Now you lie here while I get you some warm milk. Don't worry about anything."

"Grant accused me of taking cocaine. Why would he do that?"

"I have no idea, but it's obvious he's not capable of being reasonable right now. When we get back to Colorado Springs, I think you and Scotty should move home with us for a while."

Tess's hands gripped the coverlet. "Oh, Mom, I'd give anything for this not to have happened. I wanted to get off the drugs and find an apartment for Scotty and me before I asked him for the divorce."

"After what I saw and heard tonight, it's my opinion that Grant's inability to deal with your medical problem has brought your marriage to a total impasse. It wouldn't be wise to live under the same roof any longer."

"DR. MILHOUSE? Thanks for calling me back. I thought I wouldn't hear from you before lunch."

The clock said 9:30 a.m. "Your calls take top priority, Grant. Go ahead. Was I right about your wife?"

"Yes. Yesterday afternoon I took your advice and drove up to the cabin to surprise her, but she wasn't there. Mrs. Jenner claims she and her father had gone skiing and then out to dinner. When she finally did show up around eleven, she was with her father all right—though I doubt that's who she was with all day. She looked sick and said she had food poisoning, but I didn't buy it. I recognize the signs of someone coming down off drugs.''

''Describe her symptoms.''

''She was pale, clammy, and threw up three times that I know of. Every time I looked in the bedroom, her body was shaking the bed. Then she'd build up to a wild uncontrollable frenzy and would run to the bathroom.''

''Does she know you suspect drugs?''

''I accused her of taking them. Tried to get the truth out of her. She pretended she didn't know what I was talking about.''

''Did you discuss the possibility of a drug problem with Dr. Jenner?''

''Yes, but my father-in-law refused to listen and told me to leave.''

''Hmm. Obviously he's in denial about his daughter's addiction. You could try talking to Mrs. Jenner.''

''No way.''

''How about her brother?''

''Winn and I have never been exactly friends. Even if he knew she was on drugs, he'd never admit it to me.''

''What about her friends?''

Grant released an exasperated sigh. "Her best friend is married and lives in California. Tess wouldn't confide in anyone else."

"Yet she met someone in Hawaii and came home in exceptionally high spirits." He paused. "Unless you can catch her in the act, we'll have to wait for her next appointment—I'll be testing her for drugs then. If my suspicions are correct, I'll call you, and we'll discuss how to proceed from there."

"That's ten days from now, Howard. Isn't there any way you could intervene sooner?"

"Only under a court order."

"What do you mean?"

"Well, if you were to file for divorce on the grounds that your wife is an unfit mother and constitutes a danger to your child, I could supply you with the documentation. A judge could demand she submit to a drug test. Based on the outcome, he might take your son away from her temporarily until there was a full-scale trial. I suppose the right attorney could get you in to see a judge before the ten days were up."

"I—I hadn't thought about divorce...."

"Look, if divorce doesn't appeal to you, you could wait until I obtain the proof we're looking for, and then have her committed. Either way, as her husband you're in control of her. It's your call. Let me know what you decide, Grant."

"I'll get back to you soon. Thanks."

There was a click. After hanging up the phone, Howard made a notation to put in Tessa Marsden's file:

January 21—Patient's husband phoned to say that wife displays signs of having taken drugs, but there's no proof. Will investigate further at next appointment unless husband takes legal action first to protect son from possible danger.

"MOMMY? ARE YOU STILL SICK?"

Tess heard Scotty and pushed herself upright on the big four-poster bed. She felt shaky and nauseated, and perspiration made the flannel pajamas cling to her skin.

According to the clock on the bedside table, it was after 10 a.m. So she must have slept, she realized. When was she going to wake up and feel okay?

"Come here, little guy." She held out her arms and Scotty scrambled into them.

Her precious five-year-old took after Grant's side of the family with his hazel eyes and blond hair. But where Grant's was straight, Scotty's hair had natural curl. Right now he was dressed in a green turtleneck sweater and matching ski bib, and she knew he'd just come in from outside. His cheeks were glowing and his skin felt cold.

"Does your tummy still hurt?" Scotty asked.

"I'm feeling much better this morning."

"I heard you throwing up."

"It's not much fun."

Scotty pressed his head against his mommy's shoulder. "I get scared when I throw up." He lifted his head and Tessa could see his lower lip trembling. "Where's Daddy?"

Tess gripped the edge of the down quilt. "He had to go back to work."

"Will he come here tonight again?"

"We'll see." She hugged her son. This was the part she'd been dreading ever since she'd first contemplated divorcing Grant. "Where's Nana?"

"She's in the kitchen. She let me make waffles. Do you want one?"

Bile rose in her throat. "Uh, maybe later. Right now I'm going to take a shower and then we'll go sledding."

"Goody." The relief on his face spoke volumes.

"Tell Nana I'll be out in a few minutes." She dashed to the bathroom and turned on the shower taps so no one could hear her wretch. If this didn't stop soon, she was afraid her dad would have to get her readmitted to the hospital.

A few minutes later, while she was in the shower, she heard someone calling to her. She quickly rinsed off the last of the soap and shampoo, turned off the faucet and poked her head around the end of the shower curtain. Her mother was standing in the bathroom doorway.

At sixty-five, the auburn-haired Wilma still had a lissome figure and looked terrific in ski warm-ups and a cable-knit sweater. "We need to talk," she said. "Scotty's run outside for a minute, but he knows something's very wrong between you and Grant."

Tess stepped out of the shower and wrapped herself in a huge bath sheet. "You mean he heard us last night?"

"Enough."

"Oh, Mom . . . I'll have a talk with him as soon as I get dressed." Her voice shook. "I can't put it off any longer."

"I agree. But are you up to it?"

"I don't know. I keep getting the heaves." She lowered herself onto the closed toilet seat.

"Your father says those ought to stop anytime now. I'll bring you some more warm milk."

"I think I'll throw it up."

"But you have to keep putting something in your stomach."

"I know." Tess looked up miserably. "Mom? Am I going to make it?" Her body felt electrified and jittery.

"Of course you are."

"What would I do without you and Dad?"

"What would we do without *you?*"

"I'm just a burden."

"I won't listen to that kind of talk. We've hardly seen you since your marriage. We're thrilled for this chance to spend some time with you. Now, I've put a fresh nightgown on the bed for you. I know you told Scotty you'd go sledding with him, but I don't think you're up to it yet. I'll send him to your room with the milk, okay?''

Tessa nodded. Her mother was right. How could she go sledding? Even just taking a shower had been taxing. And as much as she feared the moment when she had to sit down and explain the situation with her and Grant to her son, it was a relief to finally face it. No more secrets.

Scotty was a wonderful sensitive child, mature for his age. He deserved the truth. Paul had urged her to tell her son while she was in Hawaii, but she hadn't wanted anything to mar their vacation. Scotty had been a laughing carefree boy who played in the surf and made new friends.

It sickened her to think that his world was crumbling because of their marital problems. Grant could be fun and charming. He could also be very cold and stubborn. But no matter how upset, hurt, angry or provoked he'd been last night, he had no right to be rude to her parents.

As for his accusations about her taking cocaine, they simply didn't make sense. He didn't seem to care that Scotty was in the loft of the log cabin where there was no insulation to stifle sounds. Thank heaven her father had been there, or Grant would have left the cabin with her little boy.

Perhaps it was meant to be this way. The time for the truth had come. Now it was up to her to follow through.

A deep pain seared her being. Divorce. Something she'd never believed in—until she'd married Grant.

"MOMMY?"

Tess had just slipped the clean quilted nightgown over her head when her son entered the bedroom. "Nana says you're still too sick to get up. Here's your milk."

When she took it from him, he started to leave. "No, Scotty, don't go. We have to talk about last night."

He hesitated, then whirled around, his hazel eyes glazed with unshed tears. "How come you and Daddy don't like each other?"

She tried to swallow, but couldn't. "We like each other, honey, but there are problems that make it hard for us to live together. Th-that's why when you and I leave this cabin, we're going to stay with Nana and Grampa for a few days."

Slowly, one tear, then another, trickled down his cheeks. "Where will Daddy be?"

"Come here, darling."

He hurled himself at her, inadvertently knocking the mug out of her hands onto the bed, but she didn't care. They rocked together until his sobs started to subside.

She set her son slightly away from her and looked into his eyes. "Your daddy loves you, but he's very unhappy with me right now. A-and I'm unhappy with him. Sometimes that happens in a marriage."

"Why?"

"It's hard to explain. Do you remember the time we were building a model plane together and suddenly all the pieces you'd glued fell apart?" He nodded. "Here you'd worked so hard, spent all those hours figuring everything out, and it still went to pieces. Do you remember what you did?"

He sniffed. "I got so mad I kicked them and threw the glue stick across the room."

"Yes," she said with a rueful laugh. "Well, that's how your daddy and I felt last night. We've been working at our marriage, trying to make all the pieces fit together and stick, but it fell apart, anyway. He couldn't take it anymore. That's why he went home. He didn't want to leave you, but he couldn't stay here while he was so upset with me. So I've made a decision."

"What is it?"

She took a deep breath. "Because I want to be happy and I want your daddy to be happy, I'm not going to live with him anymore. I don't ever want him to be as upset as he was last night. Do you understand?"

"Are we getting a divorce?"

The dreaded word. "Yes."

"Brad's parents are divorced. His dad comes and gets him on the weekends."

"I know."

"Is that what Daddy is gonna do?" She heard the anxiety in his voice.

"The three of us will talk everything over so that you can be with your daddy whenever you want. He loves you, Scotty. So do I. I promise you everything will work out for the best."

She crushed her son to her again, praying that her promise would be kept.

CHAPTER THREE

"LOWELL?"

"Come in, Grant. I've been waiting for you."

Grant sat down in a chair in front of Pastor Carr's desk, feeling completely at home. He'd been meeting weekly with the pastor ever since his marriage to Tess six years before, and they'd become good friends. Grant found it easy to confide in the middle-aged family man, who successfully combined his ministry and marriage.

"Thanks for seeing me on such short notice. This couldn't wait until our basketball game tomorrow night."

"Is this about the new insurance policy you sold me?"

"No. I wish it was."

"That doesn't sound good," the minister murmured. "Did Tess and Scotty get home from Hawaii all right?"

Grant nodded.

"Tell Tess the children missed her leading the junior choir on Sunday. We'll be glad to have her back."

Grant cleared his throat. "She may not be back. That's what I've come to talk to you about."

"Why? What's happened?"

"As soon as she got home from her trip, she checked in with her psychiatrist, then she and Scotty took off again for the cabin in Vail with her parents. But there's been a new development. Her psychiatrist told me he thinks she took drugs while she was in Hawaii. I'm supposed to watch for signs of them."

Lowell frowned. "You're talking about drugs other than the ones he gives her?"

"Yes."

"That doesn't sound like Tess."

"Nothing sounds like Tess anymore. She's becoming a stranger, Lowell. But even I was skeptical until I went up to the cabin to surprise her. I thought maybe we could have a romantic evening together, but that went up in smoke. She was vomiting and trembly. Her skin was clammy. All the signs of a person on cocaine."

Lowell looked shocked. "This is dreadful. I'm so sorry. Look. As soon as I can, I'll try to get Tess to come in and talk to me, all right?"

Grant nodded gratefully.

"What are you going to do in the meantime?" the pastor asked.

"I don't know. That's why I'm here. When I tried to reason with her and get her to tell me the truth, her father interrupted us and told me to leave. He refused to talk about the fact that his daughter might be taking drugs."

"I can't believe Richard would behave that way." Lowell was visibly shaken.

"Things have gone from bad to worse. My own father-in-law told me to leave the cabin. He wouldn't let me take Scotty. I honored his request because it *was* the middle of the night, and I didn't want Scotty to see the kind of shape his mother was in at that moment. She looked terrible. It's disgusting. You wouldn't have recognized her."

Lowell shook his head. "This is incredible. When I think how hard you work, the sacrifices you've made to support your wife... well, I scarcely know what to say."

"Thanks. I appreciate that. Lowell... you counsel a lot of couples. I was hoping you could give me some advice. If she's on drugs, and I'm certain she is, Scotty shouldn't be alone with her while I'm at work."

"I can understand your concern. Obviously Tess is a very sick woman."

"You don't know the half of it. She hides everything from me, and now she's starting to hide things from Dr. Milhouse. He says I have two choices. If I can get proof of drug addiction, I could have her committed. Or I could divorce her and keep Scotty with me."

Lowell shook his head sadly. "I don't like the sound of either one, but there's no question life has been very unfair to you."

"That's an understatement. You should have heard Dr. Jenner on the phone earlier. When I asked to talk to Scotty, he said he was still asleep. He told me that next week Tess and Scotty would be staying with them at their Colorado Springs home, so I should call there if I wanted to talk to *my* family." His voice shook with anger.

"I don't like the sound of that. I'd hoped your marriage could endure, given enough time."

"I married a stranger, Lowell. Another person inhabits her body, and now she's abusing it with her parents' full consent."

"This is most unfortunate," the older man murmured. "Richard is obviously too close to the problem to be thinking rationally. The bond between a father and daughter is often very strong. But it's exactly at a time like this that everyone needs help from a higher source. Perhaps I can reason with Wilma."

"I wouldn't count on it. She's like a mother bear with her cub. Dr. Milhouse agrees that we've reached the end of the line."

Grant watched as the pastor sat back, pondering his statement. "You deserve a chance at happiness, Grant. If you have your wife committed, you'll go through life without a companion. That would be a tragedy. No man should live alone."

He steepled his fingers beneath his chin. "Of the two choices, Grant, divorce makes the most sense. Dr. Jenner has the means to care for his sick daughter. You would gain custody of Scotty and someday, I'm sure, find a woman who would be a loving wife to you and a good mother to your son."

"Yes," Grant said softly. Then more strongly, "Yes. I agree with you. So—" he took a breath "—do you know a good attorney?"

Lowell looked pensive. "I'll get my wife on the phone. Her cousin's a corporate lawyer. I'll ask her to call him and see if he can recommend someone."

"I hoped you'd be able to come up with a name. I need help right away."

"I understand. But as you know, I'm in the business of *keeping* marriages together. But don't fear— I'll get Connie to call her cousin now and then call me right back. You can wait here. Oh, before I forget— you're welcome to come to dinner tonight."

"Thanks. I was dreading the thought of going home to an empty house again."

While Lowell was busy on the phone, Grant reached for the Bible lying on the desk and thumbed through it. In a few minutes, Lowell handed Grant a piece of paper with a name and number.

"Clive Medor," Grant said musingly. "I've never heard of him."

"Neither have I, but Connie's cousin says he's one of the best."

Grant put the paper in his jacket pocket and stood up. "I really appreciate this, Lowell."

The minister smiled. "Glad to help, Grant. See you tonight, then. Sixish, Connie says."

"I'll be there." They shook hands, then Grant hurried out to the parking lot and started up his Oldsmobile.

His home was only three miles from the church, no great distance, but all he could think about was getting on the phone to make an appointment with this Clive Medor. Dr. Jenner thought his word was law. Well, dammit, he was about to find out that not everyone bowed to him.

After pulling up in front of the small ranch-style bungalow in one of the newer subdivisions of Colorado Springs, Grant ran inside and immediately went to the answering machine. There was only one message and it was for Tess. The voice was male and unfamiliar:

Hello, Tessa. This is Paul. How are you? I trust you had a good flight home with Scotty. I miss the two of you already. I wanted to let you know I've sent him that present I promised—should be arriving any day now. Tell him that for me. When it's convenient, call me at the number I gave you, okay?

"DR. MILHOUSE? It's Grant Marsden on the line. He sounds frantic. Says he has to talk to you now."

Howard told Elsa to put the call through, then asked his patient, Mrs. Dunn, to excuse him for a moment.

"Yes, Grant."

He listened as Grant told him about the message left for Tess. When Grant finished, Howard said, "This Paul is probably the one who gave her the drugs, maybe did them with her. That present might contain the proof we're looking for," he added.

"I'll watch for it."

"Can you get to my office in an hour?"

"Yes. By that time I'll have made an appointment with the attorney my pastor recommended."

"Who is it?"

"Clive Medor. Ever heard of him?"

Howard smiled. "Oh, yes."

"Is he good?"

"He has a reputation for winning cases."

"That's all I wanted to hear. Thanks for fitting me in."

"Anytime."

TESS FELT as if she were jumping out of her skin. "Dad... I think I'm going to die."

"It'll pass, honey. Just hold on to my hand and keep walking."

"I—I can't."

"Yes, you can. Take big deep breaths. Come on now."

"I'm going to be sick."

Her dad held her while she leaned over and retched in the snow.

"Here." He handed her some tissues to wipe her mouth when she was through. "Better?" he asked tenderly when she lifted her head.

"I need to lie down."

"It'll be more beneficial to keep walking. You can do it."

"The ringing in my ears is driving me crazy!" she cried. "I feel like there's a volcano erupting inside me."

"It'll pass." His calm voice soothed her. "Have a stick of chewing gum. It'll keep your jaws busy."

He unwrapped a piece and put it between her trembling lips.

"Oh, Dad...I still think I'm going to die..."

"No, honey, you won't. Trust me. You've passed through the worst of it. I'm very proud of you." He squeezed her shoulder.

Tess lost track of time as they walked. After a while she felt some of the agitation leave her body. "I'm feeling a little better."

Her father smiled encouragingly. "You're going to have more times of feeling good in between the bad now. Oh, look—I can see your mom and Scotty."

Tessa waved, then watched her son jump off his sled and run toward them. Her mother trailed behind.

"How are you, sweetie?" She hugged her son tightly, hoping he wouldn't notice her trembling limbs. "It looks like you and Nana have been having fun."

"Yup. Nana's been pulling me, just like in *The Grinch.*"

Wilma chuckled. "Luckily I only had to pull one little Who."

"Nana Marsden called me," Scotty said next.

Immediately Tess's heartbeat accelerated. She exchanged worried glances with her parents. She knew Grant was angry. Was that why he had his mother call?

"What did she have to say?"

"It's Susie's birthday tomorrow. The family's going to McDonald's. She wants me to come."

Tess sucked in a breath and was grateful for her mother, who slipped an arm through hers for support.

"Do you want to go, honey?"

"Only if you go, too."

"Your mommy's still sick," her father explained. "We'll buy your cousin a present and take it to her next week. How's that?" He picked up Scotty and started walking.

"What do you think we could get her, Grampa?"

"I don't know. How about a sled like yours?"

"She has one."

"I bet she doesn't have stilts."

Tess smiled at her father, loving him, loving both her parents fiercely for their goodness and devotion.

"What are stilts?"

"We'll have your uncle Winn show you. He still has a pair. He can make some for Susie."

"Will he make some for me, too?"

"MRS. MARSDEN? Mr. Pett will see you now."

"Thank you."

With a sense of unreality, Tess entered the office of the man who was going to be her attorney. Except for the fact that he'd gone bald at the crown since she'd last seen him at one of her parents' Christmas parties, nothing else about Milo Pett had changed.

He grinned when he saw her and extended a hand for a hearty shake. "Good to see you, Tess. You're looking more beautiful than ever. Please. Sit down. What can I get you? A Coke? Perrier?"

"Nothing, thank you." Though the vomiting had finally stopped, she still felt queasy most of the time and preferred yogurt to anything else.

He perched himself at the corner of his desk and eyed her with concern. "I'm always happy to see any of the Marsdens, but I must admit I was surprised and saddened to hear you needed my help."

"No one is sadder than I am."

"Don't be offended if I tell you I can see the stress."

She gave him a wan smile. In the elevator she'd suffered another anxiety attack. She'd gone to the rest room and stayed there until it subsided.

"I'm not offended. It's been . . . tough. But hopefully we'll all be better off after the divorce."

"You have a son. . . ."

"Yes. Scotty. He's five, going on six."

Milo Pett shook his head. "Where does the time go?" He went around his desk and sat down, putting on his glasses.

He reached for a fresh legal-sized pad of paper. "All right—" he flashed her a kind smile "—let's begin. Why are you seeking a divorce?"

"We were incompatible from the beginning, but it's grown much worse."

"Does your husband know you're going to file?"

"He probably expects me to. One night a week ago we had an ugly confrontation at my parents' cabin in Vail. I haven't seen or talked to him since because Scotty and I have been living with my folks. They've allowed him to speak to Scotty over the phone, but there's been no visitation."

"Why not?"

"Because Grant was abusive to me on the night in question. My father told him he needs to calm down. We thought it would be best to let everyone cool off until I'd had a chance to talk to you and get your advice."

He nodded. "Tell me what happened."

Trying to stay unemotional, she told him about that horrible night and then gave him as complete a picture as she could of life with Grant over the past six years. She left nothing out.

Because of Grant's unexpected accusation that she was taking cocaine, she was forced to tell Mr. Pett about her hospitalization and subsequent determination to get off all medication. But she asked him to keep that information to himself. She didn't want anyone to know about it until she'd learned for certain whether or not she was doomed to be on some sort of medication for the rest of her life.

"Now I understand the reason for those shadows under your eyes. You're a very courageous lady."

"I don't know about that, but I have to try."

"Good for you." Milo paused, then said, "How do you plan to support yourself when this is over?"

"Well, since I last saw you, I graduated in music with a teaching certificate. I've got my name in to start teaching choral music, a cappella, that kind of thing. The personnel director for the school district told me there's more than a ninety percent chance I'll be hired in the fall."

He smiled. "That's wonderful. And in the meantime?"

"In the meantime, I'm looking for part-time work and hope to find an apartment right away. I've already asked to be a teacher's aide at one of the high schools where I'm hoping to get a job. They're going to let me know next week. I told them it would have to be afternoons while Scotty's at kindergarten. I can't expect my mother to baby-sit for me.''

"Still, your parents love you and will want to support you in every way. It'll make things much easier for you and Scotty.''

"I know. But I hate being a burden.''

"I doubt you consider your son a burden. And I know your parents adore you, so enough of that kind of talk. I have three children of my own. I'd be hurt if they wouldn't let me help them out during the biggest crisis of their lives.''

"Your children are very lucky.'' She smiled. "And, I guess, so am I.''

"Do you have any problems with your husband being granted full and liberal visitation rights?''

"No. Grant's a good father to Scotty and they love each other. I don't want that to change.''

"Excellent. Okay, let's talk about division of assets.''

She and Grant had bought a small starter home and still owed most of the mortgage. And since Grant's job hadn't allowed for a lot of material acquisitions, figuring out what share she wanted didn't take much time.

"What about alimony?'' Milo asked.

Tess had talked it over with her parents. "If Grant will pay reasonable child support for Scotty, that's enough. He doesn't make a big amount of money. The insurance business has its ups and downs. I don't want to see him unduly burdened.

"I'll sell my diamond ring and use it to get into an apartment and pay a couple of months' rent. Provided I get that teaching job, by then I should've received some paychecks."

The lawyer's eyes reflected a glimmer of admiration. "Good. I'll get right on this, and your husband will be served in the next couple of days. If he doesn't have an attorney, this will force him to get one. The visitation is all spelled out, so there should be no problem."

Tess was relieved, but she could feel another anxiety attack coming on and needed to get out of there.

"Thank you, Mr. Pett. It helps just knowing that the process has started." They shook hands again and she left his office. The second the door shut behind her, she avoided the elevator and headed for the stairs. At least no one would see her in the throes of an attack.

CLIVE MEDOR turned on the tape recorder, then stood and walked around his desk to greet his prospective client.

"So, you're Grant Marsden. I recognize you from the *Theta Chi Alum* magazine. Seems you're still one of Colorado State University's most famous golfers."

Grant grinned and the two men gave each other the Theta Chi grip.

Marsden had good dress sense, Clive thought. He reminded him of someone in film or TV, but he couldn't think who. It would come to him eventually.

"My secretary tells me your father-in-law hasn't allowed you to take your son home. We'll remedy that."

"Thank God."

"Have a seat and relax. What do you drink? Soda? Coffee?"

"Coffee sounds good."

After asking Grant how he liked it, Clive buzzed Marcie and asked if she'd mind bringing in coffee for both of them. Then he sat down in the chair next to Grant, angling it to face him. A long time ago he'd discovered that his sitting behind a desk intimidated his clients.

"Now. Let's talk about your boy. Got a picture of him?"

Grant pulled out his wallet and handed a small snap to Clive.

The son was almost a dead ringer for his father. But it was the brunette in the picture that drew Clive's attention.

"Isn't there a portrait of your wife on the wall at the fraternity house? I'm on the alum advisory board and have to go up there every so often."

His client nodded grimly. "Yes. She was the Theta Chi Sweetheart the year we were married."

Her face, the way she wore her hair, reminded him of Hope Brady on the "Days of Our Lives" soap. Clive had picked up a lot of ideas watching the soap's twisted plots. The more outrageous and contorted, the better.

When his wife had dumped him for another man after only five weeks of marriage, there was a period when all he did was watch TV. Even though that was a long time ago, he was still hooked on "Days." His VCR was set to tape it Monday through Friday. At nights, when he was working on a case, he'd turn on the program. He found it helped him unwind.

This woman had more meat on her beautiful bones than Hope. She also had class written all over her. A touch-me-not look that could drive a man crazy. The kind of woman who didn't see a man unless she wanted to. The kind of woman who would *never* see him...

He raised his eyes to Grant's. "A woman who looks like her could give a man a lot of grief."

"You can say that again," his client muttered.

Marcie came in with the coffee. When she was gone, Clive handed back the picture. "No one," he said firmly, "has the right to keep your son from you. Let's talk shop."

He proceeded to get details about Tessa, and when he heard her maiden name, he couldn't help asking if she was any relation to Bruce Jenner. The Olympic decathlete was his idol. He said as much to Grant.

"I used to love to ski," Grant said. "Phil and Steve Mahre were my idols."

Clive nodded. They were talking the same language. "I hear you, Grant. What's your son's name?"

"Scotty. My father's name is Scott."

"Hey—your father wouldn't by any chance own Marsden Mattress Outlet?"

"That's right."

"What do you know? I bought myself an extra-firm Serta-Perfect there in college. Haven't had a bad night's sleep since."

Grant chuckled. "I delivered a couple of thousand of those babies working there after school."

Clive sighed. "That's the trouble with being a lawyer, Grant. Even if I had a son, I wouldn't be able to give him a job after school. So, what do you do now?"

"I own an insurance agency."

"Life?"

"All kinds."

"Make a good living for you?"

"I've got a ways to go yet."

"Don't we all. We'll work out a payment schedule we can both live with. Okay. Tell me everything from the beginning. Don't leave anything out because you don't think it's important. Let me be the judge of that." He glanced at his watch. "We've got an hour."

"HI, GOOD-LOOKIN'. What'll it be today? Pastrami on rye?"

Alex Sommerfield glanced up from the brief he was scanning and smiled at Hannah, who'd brought him a cup of coffee. The warm lively mother of five was an institution at Sol's Deli.

"Just so you don't start thinking you're too clever, I'll have a bagel with some of that cheese-veggie spread and a gallon of that stuff." He gestured at his coffee.

"Hmm. You must be in battle mode. What is it with everyone today? The doughnuts and sweet rolls are gone, and it isn't even two o'clock yet. At the rate the java's being consumed around here, we're going to run out of that, as well."

"Judge Mecham's going on vacation, so they're packing them in. Did you save me a piece of cheese-cake?"

"Don't I always?" She winked.

"Bless you, Hannah."

She put her hands on her hips and shook her head. "How come you can consume cheesecake every day and still look like one of those Navy Seals?"

"Navy Seal?" Alex grinned. For as long as he'd known Hannah, she'd been comparing him to everything from a Green Beret to a presidential body-guard. "That's your best one yet."

"Yeah, well, I saw one interviewed on '20/20' the other night. He doesn't have a patch on you. How do the girls around your office stand it?"

"As of the moment, I have an all-male staff."

Her eyes grew huge. "Are you serious?"

"What do you think?"

She frowned. "I don't know. You're a dark one, Counselor."

"Just so you won't turn on me and serve sauerkraut when I'm not looking, I'll ease your mind and tell you that I'm an equal-opportunity employer. But the two women in my office got married recently and moved out of state. Their replacements just happened to be males because they had the best qualifications for the job."

"Yeah, yeah, yeah." She shook her head. "One bagel coming up."

Actually Hannah had a point. Since his divorce two years ago, he'd been besieged with well-intentioned matchmakers of both sexes and found that the all-male staff reduced that matchmaking by half.

Reaching into his briefcase for the mysterious missing tax return he intended to present as Exhibit B, he could hardly wait until two o'clock when Judge Gore reconvened the trial.

Alex was looking forward to blowing Clive Medor's latest custody case out of the water. The cocky divorce attorney came on too strong for his liking.

As a rule, Alex was friends with many of his colleagues, spent time with some of them socially after hours. But before a trial, whenever he and Clive shook hands as friendly adversaries, Alex knew there was nothing friendly about it. With each meeting, Alex had the gut feeling that the aggressive, often nasty attorney would cut his own mother's throat to win a case for his client.

Sometimes Alex had the unsettling sensation that there was a hidden agenda in that Machiavellian brain. Clive seemed to have a built-in hatred for women, which he didn't bother to hide. Alex honestly thought the man was disturbed.

In his ten years as a trial lawyer, Alex had lost two of the four cases where he'd been pitted against Clive. Both times had been where Alex's clients hadn't told the truth from the beginning.

That he could be so colossally deceived by the people who'd retained him to represent them had come as a personal blow. In both instances, Clive had wasted no time in mercilessly baiting Alex every chance he got, whether in the elevator, walking out the front doors of the building or sitting in adjoining booths at Sol's Deli.

After his second loss to the man many in his profession jokingly, and not so jokingly, called "the little Hitler," Alex vowed that no client in the future would ever do that to him again. He didn't care how long the background check took.

Two hours later, elated after his victory against Clive—the Cheshire-cat grin always gave him away— Alex strode to the elevator, anxious to get back to the office and return the flood of calls that would have accrued while he'd been in court.

When it looked like it might be a long wait, he opted for the stairs.

"Wait up, Counselor."

Alex paused at the first landing and looked over his shoulder to see Clive Medor's short chunky frame negotiate the steep flight of stairs in record time, bulging briefcases in both hands.

"You didn't give me a chance to congratulate you on that neat piece of evidence."

"I'm in a hurry, Clive." Alex continued on down the stairs.

"So am I. I've got a whopping new custody case that's going to set a precedent in this state."

"Is that right?" Alex gritted his teeth and emerged from the stairwell onto the main floor. "Does that mean all the mothers going for custody should now lie down and die?"

"It bugs you that I'm changing people's perceptions of the supposedly sacrosant institution of motherhood, doesn't it."

Alex wheeled around and stared at Clive, as repulsed as ever by the other man's brushlike mustache. "No. It scares the hell out of me that you enjoy it so much."

CHAPTER FOUR

"TESS? IS THAT YOU?"

"Yes, Mom. Guess what? I got the teacher's-aide job and I start tomorrow. Where are you?"

"In the study."

There'd been a snowstorm in the night, and it took Tess a minute to unzip her boots and dispense with her parka. After hanging it up in the closet of the back entry hall, she hurried through the house in her stocking feet to find her mother and tell her the details. The paycheck wouldn't be huge, but at least she'd be able to buy groceries and any items needed for Scotty.

The large modern wood-and-glass structure built in the woods overlooking Colorado Springs was one of her brother's best designs. Following his parents' specifications, Winn had created a place in which nature did most of the decorating.

Tess found it miraculous that no matter where she turned, her gaze met with trees and sky. It was like living outside, yet one could enjoy all the creature comforts and be assured total privacy.

Anxious to find out if there'd been a phone call from Grant—he must have been served his papers by now—she dashed up the half flight of stairs to the book-lined study.

She saw her mom hunched over the desk. ''Mom?'' she cried in alarm. ''Are you sick?''

Her mother raised her head and stared at her with tormented eyes.

''No, darling, I'm fine. But Milo called. He had some bad news for us.... I wish there were some way to shield you.''

Tess's heart started to fibrillate the way it did when she had one of her anxiety attacks, which were, thank heaven, growing less frequent. She sat down hard on one of the two moire silk love seats.

''Shield me? From what?''

Wilma straightened and took a deep breath. ''Grant was served papers, but he's countersued for full custody of Scotty on the grounds that you're an unfit mother.''

''*What?*''

''There's more, darling. Milo says that after reading all the particulars, they have such a strong case he can't in all good conscience represent you and do you justice.''

''Mom, you can't be serious!''

''Unfortunately I am. Milo suggests that as soon as possible, you try to find a high-powered attorney who deals exclusively in custody-suit battles. He refuses to charge you for the office visit or the serving of the papers.''

Wilma sighed. "I tried to reach your father, but he's still in surgery. Winn is on his way over. Scotty'll be home from school in a few minutes, so I'm glad you came in when you did—we don't want to upset him with this news."

Tess was in shock. For a minute the world reeled and she clung to the armrest like a life preserver.

"Oh, darling," her mother said. "I'm sorry to give you such terrible news. It's—"

"Mom. It's me!" Winn called from another part of the house.

"We're in the study," she called back.

Tess's older brother breezed into the room, the image of her father in his younger days. Tess was already on her feet, and she threw herself into his arms.

"Hey, Tessie...what's wrong?" He set her a little away and met her gaze directly. "What did Grant do this time?"

Incapable of speech, Tess sank onto the love seat again and listened as her mother repeated the news.

"What are these 'particulars'?" he asked angrily when his mom had finished.

Tess answered him. "I've known for years that Grant thinks I'm insane. That's his favorite word for anyone who needs to see a psychiatrist. He...he doesn't believe in them. No one in his family does."

"What are they? Living in the last century? Jeez, they need to join the real world. Thousands, millions of people consult psychiatrists every day of their lives, and they're not insane." Tess loved Winn for his fierce loyalty to her. "You sure don't back down from a divorce suit because of it. What kind of an attorney is Milo, anyway?"

Wilma got to her feet and smoothed back a strand of hair that had escaped from her twist. "Milo's a good attorney, Winn. He just doesn't think he's up to this case. Custody battles aren't the sort of thing he usually handles."

Winn's eyes narrowed. "I'm going to call my friend, Roger Thorn. He's dealt with a lot of divorce cases. Is that okay with you, Tessie?"

Tess nodded dumbly and reached for her mother's hand while they watched Winn locate the attorney's number in the phone book and dial.

All the while she listened for sounds of Scotty, her feeling of unspeakable dread growing stronger and stronger.

Unfit mother. The words repeated in her head like a satanic litany.

"Tessie—" Winn looked at her "—Roger's on the line, but he's with a client. He wants to know the name of the attorney Grant has retained."

She shook her head. "I have no idea. We haven't talked since the night he left the cabin."

"Just a minute," her mom said. "I wrote down everything Milo told me. The paper's in the drawer right in front of you."

Winn immediately opened it and found Wilma's notes. "Give me a second, Roger. Yes, here it is. Clive Medor."

Almost crushing her mother's fingers, Tess watched the muscles tighten in her brother's rugged face as he listened to his friend.

"Then who the hell can?" Winn finally said in an uncustomarily harsh tone. Tess shivered.

Grimly he murmured, "All right. Thanks, Roger. I owe you."

Without pausing for a breath, Winn phoned the number he'd just written down on the sheet. Tess could tell he was talking to someone's receptionist. The fact that her brother didn't make eye contact with her or her mother spoke volumes.

Suddenly she heard the front door open. Scotty. He could come bursting into the room any moment.

Winn replaced the receiver. "What's going on?" Tess and her mother asked at the same time. A muscle worked in her brother's jaw. That only happened when he was truly angry.

He lifted his face and stared at Tess. "It seems this Clive Medor is a real barracuda. He has a formidable reputation for helping fathers get full custody of their children. Roger says you need someone equally powerful to even the odds."

He sighed deeply. "It's going to end up costing you a small fortune, because the attorney Roger recommends doesn't come cheap."

The bands of anxiety tightening her chest made it difficult for Tess to breathe. In the distance she could hear Scotty calling to her.

"I'll go see to Scotty, Tess, while you talk to Winn." Wilma gave Tess a kiss on the cheek before disappearing from the study.

Tess buried her face in her hands. "I think it's going to have to stop right here. I don't have any money, and I refuse to involve Mom and Dad in financial concerns that have nothing to do with them."

"Then borrow it from me."

"No, Winn. I love you for offering, but you're just starting to build some savings. I wouldn't dream of taking that away."

His chest heaved. "Would you rather lose Scotty?"

She squinted at him through the tears. "Does your friend Roger really think it's that serious?"

He nodded solemnly. "The other attorneys call this guy Medor the little Hitler because he's so ruthless. He's won an impressive number of custody cases. Roger says there's only one man in Colorado who has taken him on and been successful. His name's Alex Sommerfield.

"I just spoke to his paralegal and he said you can come in for a preliminary consultation tomorrow at noon. He said it's no guarantee he'll be able to represent you. He's only taking the occasional client as it is, and he won't be able to make any kind of decision until he's talked to you at some length."

Tess let out an unsteady breath. "Dear God. I can't believe any of this is happening. I—I just got a job at the school. I'm supposed to report tomorrow at noon."

"Then you'll have to call them and tell them you can't go in until the day after. According to mom's notes, there's some kind of order concerning Scotty that has to be complied with inside of three days."

"*What?*"

"That's what it says."

"I'm going to call Milo."

She grabbed the phone directory, looked up the number and called his office. His assistant answered.

"I'm sorry, Mrs. Marsden. He's gone to the courthouse, but he said that if you called to be sure to tell you that you need to retain another attorney as soon as possible. There's an order attached."

"That's why I'm calling. What kind of order?"

"I couldn't say. But the minute you retain someone else, please call the office and we'll have a courier hand-deliver the papers to your new attorney."

"Thank you," Tess said through wooden lips and hung up the receiver.

"Oh, Winn..." She crumpled in his arms.

ALEX LET HIMSELF into the office and shrugged off his overcoat and suit jacket. He liked to come in at six in the morning before anyone else was around. He coveted his thinking time, which had to be done in total quiet and privacy.

Rolling up his shirtsleeves, he sat down at his desk and reached for the first of eight briefs laid out on the huge oak desk.

His glance darted immediately to the note taped to the telephone receiver. Alex smiled, admiring Burt's resourcefulness. It had proved to be the most effective method yet for his paralegal to garner Alex's attention when he was wading knee-deep in briefs and hated to come out of the water for any reason.

Alex—Re: *Marsden vs Marsden*
I thought you'd be interested in this one. This is the case Medor's been spouting off about, the one he says will set a new precedent for the state. The first two attorneys wouldn't touch it with a ten-foot pole. Roger Thorn told Mr. Winn Marsden, the woman's brother, you were the only one who could handle it.

Tessa Marsden will be in at noon, February 1, for an initial consultation with you. Her first attorney of record is Milo Pett (Armstrong building, Ste. 6). He's in possession of the papers served on Mrs. Marsden, January 31. It contains an order to be complied with in three days concerning the five-year-old son, Scotty.

Alex sat back in the swivel chair, absently tapping the paper against his cheek, making a mental note to give Burt a raise and his tickets to the next Denver Nuggets game.

When he heard a door open and close he called out, "Gus? Is that you?"

"No. It's Burt." The impressive paralegal whose little-boy looks prevented people from taking him seriously poked his head around the door.

"What are you doing here this early?"

"I figured you'd want the papers from Milo Pett on the Marsden case, so after I left work yesterday, I went over and picked them up. Here they are."

"You must've read my mind. When did the call come in?"

"Around three-thirty yesterday. I covered for you in the event you *don't* decide to take the case. Coffee's coming right up."

Alex flashed his right hand a smile. Burt was worth ten law clerks.

"I also did a little checking on my own, because the name Winn Jenner sounded familiar. He's the architect responsible for the remodeling of that brewery downtown, the one converted to an Old World restaurant."

Alex nodded. "He did an amazing job with that."

"I agree. I also found out the woman's father is Dr. Richard Jenner. He's an orthopedic surgeon who's a big contributor to the arts and the symphony."

Alex let out a whistle. "My ex-wife's brother, Neil, went to him when he broke his collarbone playing high-school football. I think we've got a hot one here, Burt."

He reached into his back pocket for his wallet and pulled out a couple of tickets. "Well done," he said, extending them to Burt. "Expect a bonus in your next paycheck."

Burt beamed like a shiny new light bulb. "Thanks, boss."

With a brand-new reason to hail the day, Alex immersed himself in his cases, anticipating getting his hands on Clive Medor's countersuit.

"WHAT'S THIS?"

Grant had gone out to the front porch to bring in the mail and saw the box that had been delivered. Printed on it was "The Black Pearl Gift Shop. Tradewinds Hotel, Honolulu, Hawaii." Where Tess and Winn had stayed. His eyes strayed to the label: "To Master Scotty Marsden and Family."

"Well, I'm the head of the Marsden family, so I'll open this puppy and find out what's going on."

He put the heavy box under one arm, pulled the bills from the mailbox and went back into the house. Retrieving some scissors from a drawer in the kitchen, he pried open the box, then frowned. All he could find were coconuts, pineapples and macadamia nuts. No drugs.

A small note was included: "In memory of seven wonderful days that brought me more happiness than I have known in years. Devotedly, Paul Wong."

Grant felt a surge of anger. Never once in their marriage had Tess done anything to make him think she could ever be interested in another man. Her inability to satisfy him sexually, her refusal to wear more revealing clothes, had convinced him of that.

Apparently he was wrong, and Dr. Milhouse was right. Grant should never have let Tess out of his sight. It seemed she was good for a roll in the hay, all right, just not with her own husband.

Grant's body went rigid. He'd been attractive to the opposite sex since junior high. In his freshman year in college, he'd been voted the best-looking Theta Chi and had had his pick of women.

Before graduation, there'd been an exchange with the sorority Tess belonged to. He'd met her and had fallen for her on the spot.

His fist closed over the note. To think that the Theta Chi Sweetheart had had an illicit affair with a stranger whose last name was Wong made him want to vomit.

Reaching for the phone, he called the Jenners'. "I want to talk to Scotty," he said as soon as his mother-in-law answered.

"Hello, Grant. Just a minute and I'll get him."

The ever polite gracious Wilma Jenner. Wouldn't he love to see that porcelain face crack when she learned that her daughter had been shacking up with a drug dealer. No telling what kind of dope he'd given her. What was it Dr. Milhouse had said? She was euphoric?

"Daddy?"

"Hi, partner. How are you doing?"

"Good. Winn's making some stilts for Susie and me, and I'm helping. Did you ever have stilts?"

The pencil Grant had been holding snapped. "No. I can't say that I did. Tell me about that man you met in Hawaii, Paul Wong."

"Did his present come yet?" His son's excitement caught Grant off guard.

"Yes. I hope you don't mind that I opened it, partner. Good thing I did, or it might've spoiled."

"What was it?"

"Coconuts and pineapples and nuts."

"Yum. Paul took us on some tours. He showed me how to pick out a fresh pineapple, and he taught me how to open a coconut. I have a little knife that belonged to his son. He taught me to be real careful when I use it, so I won't cut myself. It's for cutting fruit."

Grant gnawed his lower lip. "Sounds like a nice man. Did you spend a lot of time with him?"

"Every day. He owns the hotel. We could do whatever we wanted. He took us out on his own ka-ter-ran-man. It was neat. And one day he took us in a seaplane to some other islands."

Grant's fingers tightened on the receiver. "That must've been fun. How about you coming home? I want to hear more about your trip."

"Okay. Hang on. I'll go ask Nana."

After a moment, "Hello, Grant?"

"I'd like to see my son."

"Of course you would," Wilma said. "And he wants to see you. But because of what happened at the cabin, our attorney has advised us to wait until both attorneys have agreed on visitation. In another day or two this should all be settled."

His mouth stretched in a grim smile. It'd be settled all right. Clive Medor would make sure of it. Then the Jenners would come begging.

"Thanks, Wilma."

He hung up the phone, then punched in the number for his attorney's office. If Tess thought she could perform for someone other than her own husband and not pay for it, then she was very much mistaken.

Just watch me. Scotty won't be with you for long. Your pain has only begun....

ALEX STRODE OUT of his office to greet the woman Clive Medor planned to bring to her knees. To his surprise, he discovered the Jenner family en masse. They made quite an impression.

All four got to their feet when he entered. The women, obviously mother and daughter, were taller than average, possessed superb bone structure, and their clothing was simple yet elegant. The older of the two men was patrician in bearing, and his resemblance to the younger man was striking; both were tall, lean and handsome, possessed of the same glossy, dark brown hair as the younger woman. The mother was auburn-haired.

Their countenances were somber, their gazes direct and unwavering. Nine times out of ten, a client who looked Alex in the eye from the outset was trustworthy. Only twice had he been duped. That would never happen again....

Rarely in his career had he seen a family that looked so united. Like beautiful rare birds in chevron formation, they flew to an invisible signal, making them at once regal and exclusive. He imagined that exclusivity would daunt anyone less self-assured.

One by one Alex shook their hands, saving the younger woman until last. She, of course, must be Tessa. He hadn't accepted her case yet. He hadn't read through the countersuit sitting on his desk. Like a schoolteacher who preferred to ignore the reports and make his own assessment about the reputed hellion coming into his class, Alex wanted to get a sense of this woman before he saw body and soul vivisected on paper by a master butcher.

Alex had already been affected by her utterly feminine essence. What he wasn't prepared for was the electrical current that shot through his body at the touch of her slim fingers.

Impressions flew at him on several levels. Enclosed in his large one, her hand was cold, exceptionally so. He could see the pulse at her throat, and it was racing. A trace of moisture broke out along her hairline. Her breasts rose and fell rapidly. He focused on her eyes and saw her pupils dilate, almost obliterating the golden brown irises.

He knew in an instant. She was terrified.

Alex felt an involuntary stirring of his protective-male instincts. By some mysterious process of natural selection, he found himself committed. And there wasn't a damn thing he could do about it.

"You're not going to lose your son," he said, then released her hand, inclined his dark head and invited them into his office.

TESS HAD FELT the attack coming on while they'd been waiting in the reception area. When her ears started to buzz and her skin went clammy, she had to ride it out the way her father had taught her. Unlike a seizure, she was conscious, but operating on a different level of awareness.

When her heart raced too fast, she forgot to take deep breaths and found herself panting. It was in this state that she had sensed someone approaching.

Helpless, she felt her hand swallowed in an electrifying masculine grip. Unexpected warmth seeped into her cold palm and began spreading throughout her body, driving out the cold.

An awareness that she was in the presence of a power greater than she'd ever known was all the more overwhelming because her body was still fighting withdrawal.

"You're not going to lose your son."

In the midst of the volcaniclike eruption torturing her nervous system, she heard the marvelous pronouncement. Like a mortal with whom a god from

Olympus had seen fit to communicate, she continued to feel safe even after her hand was released.

"I'm here, honey," her father whispered. "Just put your arms around your old dad and hold on tight. You're going to be fine."

I know, her soul responded out of a new confidence, even if her lips couldn't form the words. She blindly obeyed the familiar voice of her parent and clung to him until the hissings and vibrations subsided.

"Take a couple of deep breaths. That's it, honey. Feel a little better now?"

Tess nodded.

"That one only lasted a few minutes. It won't be much longer before this is all behind you," her father murmured. "Come on. Mr. Sommerfield is waiting."

Humiliated to realize that someone other than her family had been witness, she whispered, "What's he going to think?"

"We're going to tell him the truth. The complete unvarnished truth. Then he won't have to think anything. He'll *know.*"

ALEX HELD the office door open for Dr. Jenner and his daughter. From what he'd just observed, Tessa Jenner was ill. Whether she suffered from some type of medical condition, be it temporary or chronic, he was about to find out.

Under normal circumstances, a person's illness would have little to do with a straightforward divorce based on incompatibility. But Alex had done some investigating ahead of time.

Two prominent divorce attorneys didn't want to touch her case, and one of them was a close personal friend of Dr. Jenner's. Alex grimaced to realize that Clive Medor probably knew more about Tessa Jenner, or thought he knew, than was humanly decent. He'd been spouting that this case would rewrite the history books.

Over my dead body, Alex vowed silently as the eyes that had communicated such terror now sought his for understanding.

CHAPTER FIVE

ALEX WAITED until everyone was seated in the leather chairs around his desk. "I've read the complaint Milo Pett served on your husband, Tessa. Do you mind if I call you that?"

"No. I'd prefer it," she replied in a melodic speaking voice Alex found extremely pleasant to the ear.

"And I prefer to be called Alex by all of you." He sat forward. "Since you've discovered that neither attorney you've approached wants to take your case, is there anything you feel ought to be changed in your complaint? Anything you should have added or deleted?"

"No," she answered automatically.

Since few people ever ran up against anyone as unscrupulous as Clive Medor, Alex could forgive her naïveté.

"Does this mean you're willing to take my daughter's case?" Dr. Jenner asked.

"That's right," Alex replied.

The older man's relief was visible. "Do you know what kind of information the attorney for Tess's husband thinks he has to assume my daughter is unfit for the task of raising Scotty?''

Beneath the man's genteel surface, Alex could tell Dr. Jenner was furious. This was only the beginning....

''Mr. Medor's only business is to make sure husbands get custody of their children in a divorce suit. For this meeting today, I don't need to know the specific contents of the countersuit delivered from Mr. Pett's office to warn you that Mr. Medor will use any means at his disposal, and I mean *any* means, to prove she isn't capable of mothering her son.''

He saw the two women reach for the other's hand and cling. The younger man exchanged glances with his father, and his mouth thinned to a hard line of anger.

Alex directed his gaze at his client. ''Do you want to tell me exactly what happened out in the reception room a few minutes ago?''

Without hesitation she said in a calm voice, ''I've been going through drug withdrawal for the past couple of weeks. Dad has been helping me.''

Drugs. He could just imagine Medor's joy. ''What kind of drugs are you talking about?''

''Allow me to answer that, Alex,'' Dr. Jenner intervened.

With a simple nod, Alex gave the go-ahead and listened to the noted surgeon. As the facts emerged, Alex's initial alarm fled. In its place grew a healthy respect for the beautiful woman who, to get off her medication, had risked death in a mountain hospital.

This Paul Wong, he realized, had a lot to do with that determination. Alex wondered if there was something in their relationship she hadn't confided to Dr. Jenner or her brother.

It was a question he would ask Tessa later, when they were alone. For reasons he had no desire to examine yet, he dreaded hearing her answer. But it would have to be asked in order to protect her in case Medor learned of Wong and decided to add adultery to the charges.

For now it was enough that Alex had witnessed her struggle for himself, seen that she was willing to do whatever was necessary to fight for her health, her sanity, her life—and her son.

Medor would be apoplectic when he found out his client's wife was not using illegal drugs as he'd no doubt charged. Far from it, she was trying to rid her body of all medication. Either way, Medor had no case.

According to Dr. Jenner, Tessa had been under her psychiatrist's care for four years and had functioned normally in the rearing of her child.

Opposing counsel would have Scotty tested by a court-appointed psychologist to offer proof he had suffered damage at his mother's hands. Of necessity, that report would also take in the father's contribution, which could be illuminating, Alex mused.

Of course the court would also order psychological testing for Tessa and her family, plus order a custody evaluation, which would include a psychiatric assessment of Tessa and require her to attend group therapy. Alex would have the evaluation put off for a few weeks until the worst of her withdrawal symptoms had subsided.

If down the road she went back into depression, they'd deal with that then. But already Alex was counting on Paul Wong's assessment of the situation—that she didn't need the drugs at all anymore. After her heroic effort, it would be devastating to everyone if she turned out to need them.

Alex included himself in "everyone," which was insane since he'd only met her an hour ago.

"Before I answer the countersuit," he said to the family, "I'd like to talk to Tessa alone. It won't take long."

Mrs. Jenner approached his desk with her son at her elbow. They both shook his hand. "My daughter has been an exemplary mother, and Scotty adores her. Why Grant would say otherwise is a mystery to me. Thank you for taking her case."

"It's my pleasure, believe me," Alex said truthfully.

Winn spoke next. "Tessie was fine until she married Grant. They were wrong for each other from the start. I've been urging her to get a divorce for ages, but our church frowns on it and she hasn't wanted to give up."

Winn's comment hit a little too close to home. Alex had put off his own divorce for similar reasons. The explanation clarified a great deal for him.

"I'll do anything to help my sister," Winn finished.

Alex smiled. "I'm counting on it." He extended his hand to him, then Tessa's father gripped it heartily. "Dr. Jenner, I'll let you know the date for the 'show cause' hearing. At that time we can discuss fees."

"Good." Dr. Jenner nodded, then ushered his wife and son from the room, stooping to kiss his daughter's forehead on his way out.

Once they were alone, Alex sat down and buzzed Burt. They needed something to drink. When he asked Tessa her preference—coffee, perhaps, or Coke?—she asked for ginger ale.

His lips quirked. "No caffeine, either?"

"No." Miraculously she returned his smile.

Lord, she was breathtaking, like some Russian princess with her great eyes, high cheekbones and sculpted mouth. He'd never met a woman who could pull her hair starkly away from her face like that in a high ponytail and still be so flawlessly lovely.

He gave Burt their order, then turned to Tessa and thrust to the heart of the issue.

"Who talked about divorce first? You or your husband?"

"Dad told you about the night at the cabin when Grant accused me of taking drugs. My father asked him to leave and said he couldn't take Scotty with him. At that point, Grant had to know it was the end of our marriage. But—'' she paused ''—neither of us ever said the word 'divorce' out loud.''

Taking a deep breath, she explained, ''After I got home from Hawaii, I kept my appointment with Dr. Milhouse and asked him how he thought I should approach Grant about a divorce.'' Her voice shook. ''You see, he knows my husband well, and any advice he could give was bound to be helpful, I thought.''

''And?'' Alex prompted.

''He told me not to say anything to Grant until he'd had a chance to talk to him one more time.''

There was a knock on the door, and Burt hurried in with their drinks. When he was gone, Alex asked, ''Did the doctor make a habit of talking to your husband alone?''

She nodded. ''After my appointments, he would get in touch with Grant privately.''

''Why didn't he see both of you at the same time?''

''I always wondered that, too.''

Alex had his own ideas on the subject but kept them to himself for the time being.

He picked up his coffee, took a sip, then asked, ''Do you know if your husband spoke to Dr. Milhouse after your last appointment with him?''

''No, but I can only assume he did.''

Alex assumed the same thing and didn't like what he was thinking.

"Have you ever discussed the idea of divorce with anyone outside the doctor or your family?"

She shook her head. "No."

"Not even a close friend?"

"No."

"How about your clergyman?"

"Definitely not."

"Why? A lot of people use clergymen for sounding boards."

Tessa took a deliberate swallow of her ginger ale, then set the glass back down and said, "My father always taught me and Winn that what went on between a husband and wife was private. He said that clergymen were not qualified psychiatrists, therefore they weren't in a position to counsel troubled marriages. Their one and only assignment was to make sure both parties felt loved by God and could count on Him for support."

The more Alex was learning about Dr. Jenner, the more he admired the man and his philosophy.

"Tessa...what do you think is the main reason for the breakdown of your marriage?"

She picked up her glass and took another swallow of ginger ale. "I know I'm far from perfect, and certainly the postpartum depression put a huge cloud over our marriage. But as soon as I was diagnosed as manic-depressive and given drugs to take, Grant started treating me like a child, like...I wasn't all there."

"Until your baby was born, did you have a happy marriage?"

"No," she confessed. "I—I couldn't seem to fill his expectations. I cried a lot, which he hated."

She sighed and looked up quickly, then away. "He made demands on me to be social, but I was still attending college. He said the best way to pick up business contacts was to parade his wife at his side. Everything he did was in excess—the partying, the late nights. It was hard to keep up my grades. He'd take me shopping and pick out clothes I would never consider wearing. He wanted me to dress in flashier clothes so I'd . . . stand out."

She met Alex's gaze squarely now. "We fought over everything, including having a baby. Before our marriage, he told me he was eager to start a family, but in reality, I had to beg to get Scotty." She paused and smiled slightly. "He's been my one great joy."

Alex digested the tragic facts with disgust. He asked Tessa about her and her husband's education, Grant's business, how she felt about their house. She told him that when they'd closed on their modest home in a new subdivision, she'd made a special dinner to let him know how happy she was.

"He sat down to eat," she continued "and I assumed everything was fine until he said, 'You can stop pretending how thrilled you are. I know you'd rather be in a house your brother designed on a piece of expensive lakefront property, but that isn't going to happen because you married *me*.'"

She managed to inject a tone that probably sounded like her husband. Alex had no problem imagining how the words must have hurt her at the time.

"*Would* you have been happier on a piece of lakefront property designed by your brother?"

Her eyes were candid. "At the time, no. We were a struggling young couple like all struggling young couples. I knew that one day, if we worked very hard, we could begin to have the things everyone dreams of.

"I was perfectly content with the little house we'd purchased. I could hardly wait to make it into a home and fix a room for Scotty. After the apartment we'd started out in, the house was heaven."

Her answer told Alex one very important thing: Grant Marsden was intimidated by the family he'd married into; he resented their wealth and status. The man would always carry a chip on his shoulder.

"Do you think your husband is still in love with you?"

"I don't know that Grant was *ever* in love with me. When we met, he wanted me, but he didn't know who I was beneath the exterior. For that matter, I didn't know who he was, either. With hindsight, I can see we were both tremendously let down."

She picked up her ginger ale and took another sip, and not for the first time, Alex noted how lovely her hands were, how slender and white and perfectly, but not flashily, manicured they were, despite what she'd been through. He raised his eyes to her face as she went on.

"My honest opinion is that after six years of unhappiness, he gets some kind of sick enjoyment out of knowing I have to take medication to survive. It puts him in a position of power—which I believe Dr. Milhouse encourages."

"You resent your psychiatrist?"

"I despise him."

Alex's brows lifted. "Does he know that?"

"I'm sure he does, but it makes no difference because I'm never going to see him again. If I find myself falling back into depression, I'll choose a new psychiatrist."

"Tell me more about Dr. Milhouse."

With that invitation, Tessa unloaded four years' worth of suppressed pain about the manipulative doctor who'd had such a stranglehold on her life.

"When I got home from Hawaii, he asked me if I'd met a man. That question made me explode. I honestly think that there's something wrong with him."

After what he'd heard, Alex agreed with her. "Did he ask you that question *after* you told him you were going to get a divorce from your husband?"

"Yes."

"Did you tell him about Paul Wong?"

"No. I refused to dignify his question by answering it. I've been his patient for four years!" she blurted passionately. "He should know I would never even *look* at another man. For him to suggest such a thing seemed a total betrayal of our doctor-patient relationship.''

"But you did meet a man," Alex persisted, his eyes narrowed.

"Yes, and he's old enough to be my grandfather."

"Grandfathers aren't too old to have affairs."

"Not this grandfather!" she retorted. "Not with me!"

That was all Alex needed to hear. He drained his coffee and asked, "How's Scotty handling what's happened?"

At the mention of her son she became more emotional. "He's not quite six, and so little. Right now he accepts what I tell him and he's very sweet about everything, but I'm not deceived. I know he must be confused and frightened. Ever since we've been staying at my parents, he wants to sleep with me."

"Does he cry for his father?"

"No, but he talks about him, and I know he wants to see him. He doesn't seem to want to be alone with him since that scene at the cabin."

Alex knew she wasn't going to like what he was about to say. "He's going to have to be alone with him. That's part of visitation. There's a stipulation, in fact, that your husband have him for this weekend, starting at 5 p.m. Friday."

She looked aghast. "The whole weekend?"

"It's common for the father to have the children every other weekend and one evening a week, plus every other holiday, six weeks in the summer and Father's Day.''

Her eyes brimmed with unshed tears. ''What if Scotty cries and doesn't want to go?''

''It's up to you to help him. The court expects the mother to honor the father's right to time with his child. If you can make visitation a pleasant experience for Scotty so he wants to go with his father, it'll look better and go better for you when the judge hears your case.''

He gave her a moment to digest that, then said, ''Your husband's attorney will use it against you if he feels you are doing anything to keep Scotty from his father or trying to alienate his affections.''

Her beautiful face looked stricken. ''I would never do that.''

''Maybe not, but millions of women do, some with good reason, others with none. Once we go to court, Scotty will be ordered to undergo a battery of psychological tests to determine his stage of development and so on. You're going to have to prepare him to deal with all these experiences, and there'll be times he won't be able to be with you.''

''But he's so young!''

Alex could feel her anguish. ''It doesn't matter. At one point the judge will call Scotty into chambers. Behind closed doors he'll quiz your son. If you've honestly done everything in your power to help him be with his father through this difficult period, the judge will be able to tell, and in the end he'll grant custody in your favor."

Her eyes welled up with tears and she put her head in her hands. "This is a nightmare."

"Not if you remember you're doing this to keep your son." He handed her a box of tissues.

She pulled out a couple, wiped her eyes and after a moment said simply, "You're right."

"Okay, then," Alex said. "I'll go ahead and answer the countersuit. Next, a date will be set for a preliminary hearing with the judge. You plan to have Scotty ready to go with his father day after tomorrow at 5 p.m. If you ever have questions, call the office and leave your number. I'll get back to you."

"Thank you, Mr. Sommerfield. I'm very grateful. You'll never know how much."

"The name is Alex," he reminded her, opening the door.

"Alex," she said quietly.

"One last thing, Tessa. I don't want anyone to know you went off all medication and were hospitalized until we go to trial. The court needs to understand your withdrawal from medication was planned *before* your husband's countersuit. Otherwise Medor might accuse me of using a last-minute tactic to turn this case around."

Tessa nodded in agreement before leaving his office.

The scent of her shampoo remained in the air as he watched her disappear down the hall to the reception area, where her family waited. For no accountable reason he felt an unfamiliar sense of loss. Burt must have seen her leave because he buzzed Alex, not giving him any time to contemplate the strange state of his emotions.

"Boss? Are you ready to take calls? Boss?"

"Just a minute, Burt."

What was it about the name Milhouse Alex couldn't shake? He had a gut feeling, which was the only sort of feeling he acted on these days, that the name had once come up in conjunction with another client, maybe as far back as six, seven years. But which one?

"Burt..."

"Yes, sir?"

"Clear my calendar for the next three days. Gus'll handle any problems. Don't bother Steve unless you have to—he's still home recovering from back surgery. Get me on a morning flight for Honolulu, open-ended. Then dig into my files dealing with child-custody suits only. You'll be looking for a reference to a Dr. Howard Milhouse, a psychiatrist, somewhere in the depositions. Start back eight years and move forward. There's a bonus in it for you if you've found what I want by the time I get back from Hawaii."

"I'll find it, boss."

Alex never had any doubt. "Terrific. Now I'm off to court and should be back in two hours."

"Sadie's on the line."

"I can't take the time right now." Switching off the intercom, he reached for his briefcase and left his office through the back entrance. Sadie Ness would have to wait. She'd been his friend since childhood. He'd introduced her to her husband and been best man at their wedding.

He loved her, but she never gave up on anything. Since his divorce, she was determined he would meet his soul mate at one of the little dinner parties she and Ralph gave on a regular basis.

Alex didn't believe in soul mates. His ten-year marriage to Betsy had had its ups and downs like most marriages, but because they were both attorneys, they understood each other's schedules better.

When they found out Betsy couldn't conceive, it hurt. However, he was prepared to adopt children and assumed she was, too. But as the months went by, she refused to listen if he even broached the subject.

Being an only child, Alex had wanted a happy marriage and everything that went with it, which meant children. He'd believed Betsy felt the same way. And she did, except—as their marriage counselor later explained to him—she was one of those women who didn't feel she could bond to another person's child. Given enough time, perhaps those feelings would change.

So Alex waited. With each year that passed, his hope for children waned. The wall between them grew a little thicker. One day he discovered that they'd drifted so far apart that the wall had become impenetrable.

Alex knew in his bones that divorce was inevitable, but he was a product of a family with strong religious convictions. The world might scoff, but he had a hard time ending something that should have lasted a lifetime.

One day she came to him. She'd met someone else. A successful businessman from Denver whose company had hired her to represent them in a big case. He was older, divorced, his children all married. He'd asked Betsy to get a divorce so she could marry him.

Their parting was swift and clean. Alex had already been through the pain and anguish earlier on. At the time of the final decree, though he would always care for Betsy, his romantic feelings for her were dead. But she had taken up space in his life. Now at the age of thirty-eight, he found that space needed filling with something else.

He'd always worked hard, but his well-meaning friends, Sadie among them, began to accuse him of being a workaholic. Maybe he was. So was Clive Medor.

As far as Alex could see, being a workaholic was the only thing he had in common with the little Hitler. It would take that kind of nonstop tenacity to beat him at his own game—because Alex planned to win.

A pair of golden brown eyes had looked to him as a savior—and brought to life something that had been lying dormant for years....

"MOMMY?"

Tess clutched the receiver more tightly. "Scotty? What's wrong, honey? Daddy only just picked you up!"

"Do I have to stay here tonight?"

Tess had to clamp down hard on her maternal instincts and remain calm. Watching Scotty walk out to the car with Grant for the whole weekend had been the hardest thing she'd ever done.

According to the countersuit, which was in Alex's hands, Grant had asked for full and liberal visitation rights until the first hearing. He wanted Scotty for the weekend. She'd been advised to comply. But no one had asked Scotty what *he* wanted.

"Sweetie—" her voice shook "—Daddy hasn't seen you for more than a week. He's missed you."

"But I want to come home." Scotty wasn't crying, but he sounded on the verge.

"He loves you, Scotty. I bet he has a whole bunch of great things planned. It'll be boring around here. Remember that new job I got helping at the high school?"

"Yes..."

"Well, I'm just going to be correcting papers for hours and hours. You'll have a lot more fun at home with your own toys and things."

"But why can't you come home, too?"

Tess didn't think she could endure much more. "We've talked about this already, Scotty. Daddy and I have decided that we're happier living apart. But we both love you to pieces."

"I sure do, partner."

Tess's eyes closed tightly. Grant had picked up the other extension at their house. He'd probably been listening to the whole conversation. It infuriated her and she wanted to shout at him to get off, but she couldn't. Alex had warned her to be the adult at all times and to consider Scotty's welfare above all else.

This was the part she'd always heard was so awful about divorces involving children. The parents' suspicions and resentments of each other, the children's being caught in the middle, desperately trying not to choose sides. It made for an ugly no-win situation.

"Say good-night to your mommy now, Scott. We're going to go to McDonald's and then we're going to go down to the mall."

"That sounds like fun, Scotty," Tess enthused though her heart was breaking. "Goodness, there are lots of little boys tonight who would give anything to be with their daddies and go to dinner and shopping together."

"Yeah. Kevin can't, 'cause his dad lives in California."

"That's right. But your daddy lives right here where we do. You can see him whenever you want."

She heard a big sigh that caught at her heartstrings. "Okay. Good night, Mommy."

"Good night, darling. I love you."

CHAPTER SIX

"CAN'T BRING YOURSELF to correct those tests?"

Tess was lying on the floor in front of the TV set in her parents' study, the school papers spread in front of her. She eyed her mom, who was sitting on the couch reading the newspaper.

"How do mothers ever live through visitation?"

"I know it's hard, honey. I'm going crazy, too. At least Scotty hasn't called again."

"That doesn't necessarily mean he doesn't want to. Grant might not let him phone again. If he was angry about the call earlier tonight, Scotty would've sensed it. I hate this, Mom."

"Honey—" Wilma was interrupted by the doorbell. "Since your father's still at the hospital, I'd better answer it."

"I'm coming with you. Maybe it's Grant with Scotty." Tess followed her mother through the house to the front door. She looked through the peephole. "Oh, Mom," she whispered. "It's Pastor Carr. I—I don't want to talk to him. Not tonight."

"Grant's probably told him the situation, honey. You weren't in church again last Sunday. You're going to have to deal with it sometime. Let's get it over with now."

Tess ran trembling hands through her hair. "You're right. Avoiding him won't make the problem go away."

Her mom greeted him cordially, then invited the minister in. His eyes immediately darted to Tess standing in the foyer. "Well, Tessa. How are you? Welcome home." He extended a hand, which she shook, noting how cold it was. The temperature outside was well below freezing. She hoped Grant had bundled Scotty up.

"Come in to the living room, Pastor. Let me take your coat." He shrugged it off and handed it to her. "Would you like something hot to drink?"

"No, thanks. I'm too full—barely finished dinner."

Her mother went ahead and lit the gas log. In a minute the three of them were seated around the square all-glass coffee table.

Every so often Tess felt the minister's eyes on her and it made her uncomfortable. Grant, she knew, was good friends with Pastor Carr.

"Well—" he crossed his legs "—I won't beat around the bush. I came to see if there wasn't something I could do to help you and Grant, Tess."

She chewed her lip, then said, "I appreciate that, Pastor. But I'm afraid it's too late. We're getting a divorce." *That hated word.*

"Grant told me. I can't tell you how sorry I am."

Tess stirred restlessly. "I tried every way I knew how to make it work, but I guess it wasn't meant to be. Now it's over. Really over."

He squinted at her. "Are you sure you tried everything?"

Tess flashed her a mother a signal of distress. "Quite sure."

"Isn't there something you'd like to tell me? Sometimes we harbor things when we need to unburden ourselves to someone who'll listen."

"My parents have been wonderful in that regard."

"But sometimes there are things we don't like our parents to know... for fear of hurting them."

"Pastor... what is it you're trying to say?" Tess asked. "We have no secrets in this house." She could tell her mother was becoming just as irritated as she was.

"I hesitate to say anything at all, but because it's so important, I feel it's my responsibility." He turned and stared hard at Tess's mom. "Wilma, are you aware Tess has been taking drugs?"

"What I am aware of is that Grant *thinks* my daughter has been taking drugs on top of her medication," she snapped. "But it isn't true."

"Denial isn't going to help things, Wilma. Grant has a major concern about Scotty's safety. I can understand why."

"My mother has just told you I'm not taking drugs," Tess said forcefully. "I've never taken illegal drugs in my life! Grant jumped to conclusions when he saw me throwing up at the cabin. What he didn't realize was that I had a case of food poisoning on top of flu, which I didn't know was coming on."

The pastor said nothing, only continued to look pityingly at her.

Tess couldn't take any more. Inhaling deeply, she said, "Grant's upset right now, and with good reason. So am I. We're in the middle of a divorce and emotions are running high. I'm sorry he burdened you with something that isn't true, and I realize you only want to help. I'll tell you once more—I'm not on drugs and never will be. Scotty's my life and I would never do anything to hurt him."

Lowell Carr took his time responding. "Well, I can see that now wasn't a good time to come by."

Tess wasn't sure she could retain her composure. "Pastor, why would you take Grant's word over mine?"

"My dear, I'm only trying to help."

"Then be my friend, too," Tess pleaded.

"I'd like to be, if you'll let me."

"Has something about my behavior in the past led you to think I would lie about anything this important?"

"Of course not, Tess. But you do have a medical problem. Grant has worried about your depression for years. Many times people turn to drugs when they can't cope."

"You are aware, then, aren't you, that I've been on medication for my depression all those years? Monitored closely by my doctor?"

"Well—" he shook his head "—I'm not a doctor and don't pretend to be."

"Pastor, if I was on some drug like cocaine or an amphetamine, do you think I could have gotten a job at the high school—as I have?"

Wilma Jenner got to her feet, clearly telegraphing her desire that this meeting end. "My daughter has done nothing wrong, Pastor. I blame Grant for involving you in something that's no one's business but hers, Grant's and their attorneys'!"

The minister stood up and eyed her dolefully. "I'm sorry you feel that way, Wilma. I know you're only saying these things to protect your daughter. I understand. I'll let myself out."

Once he was gone, Tess shook her head in amazement and said, "Can you believe that, Mom? My own pastor!"

"If Richard had been here, he wouldn't have dared talk to us that way."

"Oh, yes, he would have," Tess muttered with conviction. "I wouldn't put it past him to call Daddy at the office. Grant's been doing a job on him for years. The man's convinced I'm a drug addict, out of my mind."

Wilma shook her head. "I wouldn't have believed it if I hadn't heard it for myself."

"It makes me wonder how many people Grant has told about my condition, how many secretly think I'm out of my mind. If the pastor has bought into it, no telling who else has."

"Don't worry about it. The people who love you know the truth. Nothing else matters."

Tess had a gut feeling that wasn't true.

Her mother turned off the gas log and they headed back to the study. Tess started to gather her things from the floor.

"Where are you going, honey?"

"I'm too upset to work. I think I'll call Winn."

Her mother's brows lifted. "Better think twice. Winn'll go on the warpath if you tell him about the pastor. Your dad'll be home in a minute and you can talk to him."

Tess pulled off the elastic band holding her ponytail. "It's so weird to realize there are people like the pastor walking around who believe such horrible things about me."

"Stop it, Tess. The pastor isn't a gossip, so I'm sure not that many people know."

"I wasn't thinking of him, Mom. I'm talking about Grant. He's always been angry. My condition couldn't have helped. I'm sure he's convinced his whole family I'm missing a few screws."

"Don't talk like that, Tess."

"I can't help it. Do you know how many people he contacts every day in the insurance business? Think of his affiliation with Theta Chi, the alums he meets on a monthly basis. All his golf buddies. I wonder if he talks about our private life to any of them."

"That's something neither of us can answer, but it isn't important."

"It's important to me if no one believes anything I say!"

She started to cry. Her mother put a consoling arm around her and handed her a tissue. After a few minutes, Tess pulled herself together. "I'm sorry," she murmured. "You don't deserve this. I think I'll go to my room and get ready for bed."

"Yes, why don't you, honey. You need sleep."

"I'm not sure I'll be able to do that with Scotty gone."

Wilma embraced her daughter again. "Aside from everything else, how are you feeling?"

"I'm all right. I haven't had a panic attack since I left Mr. Sommerfield's office."

"That's good. Do you have any idea how proud I am of you? You're so strong, Tess."

"How can you say that when I'm a total wreck?"

"A total wreck couldn't have stood up to the pastor like that. I can't wait to tell Richard."

Tess laughed in spite of her pain.

"It's good to hear you laugh. You need to do it more often."

Tess gave her mother a squeeze, then hurried to her bedroom. Tonight she was ready to jump out of her skin, but for once it wasn't because of her withdrawal from medication. She needed to talk.

There were a couple of people she could call besides Winn and Rae. But when it came down to it, the only person's voice she wanted to hear was Alex Sommerfield's.

He engendered so much trust, so much confidence, she felt as if she could tell him anything. The bond she felt with him had nothing to do with words. At some elemental, even spiritual level, they seemed to have connected from the moment their fingers touched, or so it seemed to her. Maybe she was wrong. Maybe all his clients were equally affected by his extraordinary charisma. He radiated a power and dynamism not many people had. Tess knew without having tested this new knowledge that he would always take care of everything, that he'd make her safe under any and all conditions. She didn't know how she knew this. She just did.

He said she could call him if she had questions. Could she call him with her fears?

For several minutes she vacillated, then picked up the receiver and punched in his office number. She got his answering machine, so she left a brief message for him to call and hung up.

She glanced at the clock. It was almost nine. Winn had told her he worked long hours, but it was Friday night, after all. She had no idea of his personal life. She hadn't noticed a wedding ring on his finger, but that didn't mean he didn't have a wife and family. Or a steady girlfriend. A man like Alex would never be without a woman in his life.

Then Tess found herself wondering what kind of woman. Why couldn't she have met him when she was going to school? Well, no, he was older, so that meant he was already an attorney when she was in college. But that was a long time ago; and now she was twenty-seven, no longer a schoolgirl.

Stop it, Tess. How could she be thinking of another man, her attorney, no less, when she was still married and embroiled in a nightmare?

She hurried into the bathroom and took a shower, hoping it would relax her a little. Deep down, she had this niggling fear that Scotty was going to call in tears. She didn't know how she'd handle it if he begged to come home tonight and she had to tell him he couldn't.

She must have been psychic, because just as she was pulling on a clean nightgown, the phone rang. She flew across the room to answer it.

"Mom?"

She shuddered with anxiety. "Hi, darling. Aren't you in bed yet?"

"No. Guess what?"

"What?" He sounded happy. Her relief was so exquisite she sank down on the side of the bed.

"When we came home from the mall, I got to cut up coconuts!"

She frowned. "Coconuts? Did you buy some while you were out shopping?"

"No." He giggled. "Mr. Wong sent them to us."

"You're kidding!"

"He sent a big box with coconuts and pineapples and nuts."

"How sweet of him. Do you know when it came?"

"The other day. I've been showing Daddy how to cut them with my knife."

"Will you put Daddy on the phone for a minute?"

"Okay." She heard him call Grant.

"What is it, Tessa?"

"I understand a present came from Hawaii."

"From the Tradewinds Hotel, compliments of Mr. Paul Wong. Who's he?"

"The man who owned the hotel. He was crazy about Scotty. Did he send a letter?"

"A note was stuck inside."

"Would you mind reading it to me?"

"I'm not sure what I did with it. In essence it said something about having had a wonderful time with you and Scotty. That's about it."

"Thanks, Grant." She fought to keep the sarcasm out of her voice. "How's it going with Scotty?"

"How do you *think* it's going?" he challenged. "I am his father, after all."

"Grant, I'm not intentionally trying to upset you."

"I know. You just do it naturally. You want to say good-night to Scotty?"

"Unless he's asking to, maybe we should just let it alone."

"Good idea. See you Sunday night." The phone went dead.

"Who was that, honey?" Her mother came into the bedroom.

Tess replaced the receiver. "Scotty. But he was happy. Apparently Paul Wong sent a gift of coconuts and pineapple the other day, and I'm only finding out about it now. If Scotty hadn't said anything, Grant would never have told me. As it is, he seems to have misplaced the note Paul enclosed."

"Given the state of affairs, does that really surprise you?"

"Yes. If I'd received a gift for Grant, I would've made certain he knew about it immediately."

"But that's the difference between you two. Grant is—"

"Angry." She finished for her mother. "I know. Isn't that the most convenient excuse you've ever heard? No matter what Grant does, it's okay because he's angry, as if that somehow exonerates him and makes him a decent human being like the rest of us."

Her mother started clapping and grinning from ear to ear.

Tess shot her a perplexed glance. "What?"

"I do believe the old Tess has come back to life."

"What do you mean?"

"I can tell you're not on medication anymore. It's wonderful. You're animated, natural, exactly the way you were before you got married. I saw it tonight when you stood up for yourself in front of Pastor

Carr. I'm sure he didn't have the faintest idea what to make of you."

Wilma moved closer to Tess and placed her hands on her shoulders. "Before, while you were on medication, you would've been disturbed, but there was always this...passivity about you. Tonight there was fire in your eyes. Keep this up, and I believe the only drug you'll ever need again is maybe aspirin for a headache."

"Oh, Mom, do you really mean it?"

"Absolutely. You're starting to act and sound like your old vivacious self, and I see no signs of depression. The transformation has been going on little by little since that night in Vail. Tonight I can say there's a miraculous change in you."

"You know," Tess murmured, "even though I still have anxiety attacks, most of the time I feel wonderful. I can't believe I'm saying that when my life has never been in a more precarious state. But to know that Grant and I don't have to live under the same roof is so liberating I could jump for joy."

"So could I. Whatever was wrong with you a long time ago is over. It's gone. Honey, it's a great blessing and *you* made it happen!"

"It *is* over. Even *I* can tell." The most telling sign of all was her preoccupation with Alex Sommerfield, but she kept that to herself. "I—I used to feel as if I was wrapped up in cotton swabbing, like there was this shield around me. That feeling has totally gone."

She threw her arms around her mother and they hugged.

"No more blood tests, Mom."

"No more Dr. Milhouse. I must confess I never cared for him."

"*Now* you tell me." Tess laughed.

The phone rang. "Scotty?" they both said together.

"I'll get it." Tess hurried to the phone. "Hello?"

"Tessa?"

She knew that deep vibrant voice. It came right through the phone and invaded her body all the way to her toenails. *Dear God.* What was happening to her?

"Mr. Sommerfield." The use of his surname was deliberate. She didn't dare start thinking of him as Alex.

"My paralegal said you called. How are you?"

"F-fine." She should never have phoned him. "I didn't expect you to call tonight. It wasn't an emergency. Forgive me if I've intruded on your privacy. You have a right to be home with your wife and family without worrying about interruptions." She might as well find out the bad news right away.

There was a pregnant pause. "I gave you permission to call me anytime. For the record, I'm divorced and have no children, so you needn't fear you're disturbing my nonexistent personal life."

Her hand tightened on the receiver till her wedding ring cut into her skin.

"Right now I'm in the lobby of the Tradewinds Hotel in Honolulu getting ready to go to dinner with Paul Wong."

She blinked. "You're kidding! Hawaii? You're going to be with Paul?"

"Uh-huh. Do you have a message for him?"

"Yes," she said, but it came out more like a croak. "Tell him thanks for the lovely gift. Scotty's having the time of his life cutting things up with the knife that belonged to Paul's son."

"I'll tell him."

"Alex...I never saw the box or the note. I got all this from Scotty and Grant. When I asked Grant to read Paul's note to me, he said he couldn't find it."

"That's because he turned it over to Medor."

She swallowed hard, only now beginning to realize what she was up against. Thank God for Alex.

"Would you tell Paul something else for me?"

"Of course."

"Please tell him his theory was right. Whatever was wrong with me has righted itself. I'm off the drugs and experiencing no depression. Thanks to him I'll never go on them again. One day I'll thank him properly."

Another pause. "That news has made my day and our case." Though thousands of miles separated them, she could hear excitement in his voice.

Trembling, she said, "I know how important this is, particularly since my pastor dropped by the house earlier tonight. He's fully convinced I'm a drug addict."

"So that's why you called."

"Yes." *That's part of it, but the rest I can't tell you because I don't understand it myself. I just had to.* "He wouldn't believe Mother or me."

"Remember, a clergyman is still just flesh and blood."

She shuddered. "He and Grant are close friends and I'm afraid a lot of damage has been done. In fact I'm pretty sure that anyone who knows Grant believes I'm not all there."

"I have news for them," was all he said, but again she heard something alive and vital in his tone that made her pulse erratic.

"But what if he convinces Scotty I'm crazy? Who knows what construction Grant has put on my friendship with Paul?"

"One of the reasons I'm in Hawaii is to get testimony from him, and some sworn affidavits from the staff and others testifying to the times and places you were seen with Paul. I'm certain Medor will try to pin an adultery charge on you."

Tess's heart plummeted. She was rendered speechless.

"Tessa?"

"Uh-huh?"

"It's routine for Medor. Don't worry about it. I'm anticipating anything and everything so we'll be ready for him."

Sucking in a deep breath, she said, "What do women do who don't have representation like you?"

"I'll take that as a compliment."

"It was meant as one."

"Tessa . . . as long as I've got you on the phone, I want you to do me a favor. Get together with your family and make a list of people who came in contact with you after your baby was born. Anyone you can think of who might have witnessed your depression. It was five years ago and our memories don't always serve us that well. That's why several heads are better than one. When I get back to Colorado Springs, we'll go over that list."

"I'll get right on it."

"Good. How is the visitation going?"

"Well—" she glanced at her watch "—it's only been about five hours. Scotty phoned a little while ago, and so far he seems to be handling it."

His low chuckle thrilled her. "That's good. You must have prepared him well."

"I had a good coach," she couldn't resist telling him. "Thank you for calling me back. I feel much better. Have a lovely evening."

"Aloha, Tessa."

Aloha. It hadn't been very long ago she'd heard that word. She and Scotty had been walking through the Honolulu airport draped in orchid leis.

Suddenly an image of Alex came to mind. Dressed in a summer suit, at least six foot three, strong and powerful—with a lei around his neck accentuating his midnight brown hair, reflecting in his dark fringed eyes, which were as blue as the Pacific.

The receiver was still clutched to her breast when she heard her mother, who'd been sitting on the bed the whole time, give a little gasp.

Instantly she replaced the receiver and whirled around. As their gazes met, Tess felt the blood creep up her neck and into her face.

"I have eyes in my head, Tess."

Tess was mortified. "Am I that transparent?"

Her mother smiled and nodded. "I can safely declare that Paul Wong's suggested cure has been one thousand percent effective." She got to her feet and planted a kiss on her daughter's cheek. "Good night, darling."

"GRANT? THANKS FOR COMING in on your lunch hour."

"No problem, Howard." He sat down opposite the desk. "Did Tessa keep her appointment yesterday?"

"No. That's what I wanted to talk to you about. All I'm getting is an answering machine at the Jenner house. Her blood levels need to be checked every two weeks."

"Call her father at work."

"I'll do that if I can't reach her any other way. When was the last time you saw her?"

"Today's Tuesday. I saw her Sunday night when I took Scotty back."

"What was her condition?"

"She wasn't throwing up, if that's what you mean."

"Did she act euphoric, exceptionally excited?"

"Yes. You'd have thought she and Scotty had been separated three years, instead of three days. If she'd ever once in the last four years acted that happy to see me..."

"Drugs can alter a person's behavior drastically. Have you had any luck finding them among her personal effects?"

"No. And unfortunately the Jenner home is a fortress, and I'm not exactly a welcome guest who can walk in there and search her room for evidence. Last weekend Pastor Carr went over to see what he could find out, but she denied everything. So did Wilma. I guess the only way to know the truth is to get her in for tests."

"Since your wife's never not kept an appointment before, it leads me to believe she's afraid of what I'll find. I don't mean to alarm you, Grant, but if she's combining drugs with the medication she's on, she shouldn't be alone with Scotty."

"I've already told my attorney all that. He's working on it."

"You sound down. Anything particular you want to talk about?"

"What's there to say? My wife's been unfaithful and takes drugs. I can't trust her to be alone with my son anymore, and I have to wait until tomorrow to see him again. Life can't get much worse than that."

"Do you have family support?"

"Oh, yes. My folks are letting me move in with them this weekend. My attorney says I'm going to win custody, so we're fixing up one of my brothers' old rooms for Scotty. Mom'll tend him when I'm at work. After the preliminary hearing, we'll be taking him home for good."

"What's the date of your hearing?"

"I find out today."

"Is your wife going to remain in the house you bought?"

"No. She's staying at her folks. I'm going to rent our house out to some people I know until the divorce is final. My attorney's going to cost me an arm and a leg."

As soon as Grant left, Howard buzzed his nurse and asked her to get Dr. Richard Jenner on the line at the orthopedic clinic. Moments later, Elsa told him that Dr. Jenner was in surgery and would have to return the call later.

While Howard waited for his next patient, he made an entry in Tessa Marsden's file:

February 6—Patient did not come in for blood test. Is now one day late. Continue to believe patient is on drugs and intends to avoid office visit. Have warned husband of danger in leaving child alone with mother. Am trying to reach patient's father to warn him of danger to his daughter's health. Have sent report on patient to her husband's attorney.

CHAPTER SEVEN

"DR. JENNER and Mrs. Marsden are here."

Alex glanced at his watch. Two-thirty already. "Give me one minute, Burt. Then send them in."

Alex rose from his desk and went through a connecting door to the suite's small kitchen. Since his return from Hawaii yesterday, he'd kept Paul Wong's gift for Tessa in the fridge, anticipating today's meeting.

But as he started for the door, a strange compulsion made him undo the lid and pull the two leis from the tissue. By the time he returned to his office, his client and her father had entered the room.

He nodded absently to Dr. Jenner because his gaze had already fused with a pair of startled golden brown eyes. "Aloha from Paul," Alex murmured. He placed the profusion of pink and white orchids over her head and felt her silky ponytail tangle in his fingers. He had an inexplicable urge to free every lustrous strand from its confinement.

For a breathless moment the perfume from the flowers and her own delicious scent consumed him. A tiny gasp escaped her lips.

Lord.

"Th-They're exquisite," she stammered before averting her eyes. Her chest rose and fell rapidly. He had no way of knowing if she was experiencing another anxiety attack or reacting to the same burgeoning awareness encompassing him...

As he moved to his desk he heard her say, "Oh, Dad. I'm afraid I'll never be out of Paul's debt."

"He's proud of you, honey. You followed his advice and took the risk with miraculous results."

"Amen," Alex inserted. "Those orchids are meant to convey the joy he feels for you. If I didn't think you'd be buried alive in flowers, I would've added another lei to proffer my own congratulations. How do you feel now, Tessa?"

He hoped his question sounded casual. It was shocking how much her answer mattered to him. In all his years of practice, he'd never once become emotionally involved with a client. It was unethical, immoral. *Insane.*

"I feel good again. Normal. The way I used to feel before Scotty was born. My anxiety attacks are far less often. The last one was two days ago."

Considering the precarious nature of this case, she couldn't have given him better news. "That's good, because the preliminary hearing has been set for 10 a.m., February 16. We have work to do."

Just then there was a buzz on his intercom. He apologized for the interruption and picked up the phone. "Yes, Burt?"

"Sorry to bother you, but I finally found it!"

Alex knew exactly what he was referring to; his paralegal was worth his weight in gold. Turning in his swivel chair for privacy, he murmured, "Go ahead."

"It was the *Carling vs Carling* case."

"That was a jury trial, September, seven years ago, right?"

"Right, but Dr. Milhouse's name didn't appear on the official court transcript. I found it on a sheet from your legal pad with a list of potential jurors. Apparently during the jury-selection process, a witness you wanted to call—"

"I remember," Alex broke in. "Stephanie's mother was turned down by opposing counsel because it was discovered she was undergoing intensive psychiatric treatment at the time and wouldn't make a reliable witness."

"Yes, and Dr. Milhouse was her doctor of record."

"I knew I'd run across his name before. Is the woman's condition mentioned anywhere?"

"No. But I can find out easily enough by calling your former client."

"You took the words out of my mouth, Burt. Good work as usual. Interrupt me anytime."

Turning back to Tess, he gave her his full attention. "Have you had an opportunity to make up that list of people for me?"

"Yes, but it's probably not complete." She took a paper from her purse and handed it to him.

"It's a good start."

While Alex scanned the names and their relationships to her, he was cognizant of the fragrance from her leis. It reminded him of the time spent with Paul Wong and their discussion about Tessa and her son.

A sixty-five-year-old widower, Paul claimed to have seen a likeness to his deceased son in Scotty. Early one morning, the charming little towhead had run up to him on the beach in front of the hotel, anxious to show off a shell he'd found.

As Paul explained it, Tessa, followed by her brother and sister-in-law, came out of the water right behind Scotty, and the five of them struck up a conversation. Alex listened carefully to Paul's tone of voice. It confirmed that he found Scotty's mother as charming as the son.

Being sixty-five didn't exempt him from the possibility of wanting an intimate relationship with Tessa Marsden. There was no disputing that her beauty had an impact on everyone who met her. Despite Tessa's and Paul's sworn statements—plus corroborating evidence from eye witnesses that there was no affair—the court's reaction to Tessa's remarkable looks would work against her.

Medor would have a field day with his accusations of adultery. But Alex wasn't worried. Though the judge would take it all in, his ultimate concern would be for Scotty. Which parent would best serve the boy's interests over the formative years.

At no time in Hawaii had Tessa put her son's life in jeopardy or demonstrated neglect. The judge would have that testimony confirmed when he took Scotty into closed chambers for a talk.

The only real damage would be to Tessa's psyche. Just sitting in a courtroom with a husband who was now her most bitter enemy was bad enough, but to be labeled a drug addict and an unfit mother, as well as an adulterer, was a truly hellish experience, from which a lot of people never recovered.

But Alex had seen her tremendous fight to wean herself from all medication, and he knew she had amazing hidden reserves of strength. Medor would plumb those reserves to the last dregs and then go for the jugular. That was when Alex would go into battle mode....

Dr. Jenner stirred. "Alex? What's your advice about the situation with Dr. Milhouse? He's been trying to reach me at work. Tess missed her appointment with him yesterday. I'm going to have to call him back with an explanation."

Putting the paper on the desk, Alex's gaze darted to his client's father. "Call him and tell him it's your professional opinion that your daughter has fully recovered from her depression. Tell him she no longer requires medical treatment of any kind. Thank him for everything he's done in the past, wish him well and let that be the end of it."

Dr. Jenner looked relieved. "I'll do it as soon as I get back to my office."

"Good." Alex nodded and turned to Tess. "Now, I want to hear in detail what happened after you gave birth to Scotty, the symptoms of your depression. Help me understand how the people named on this list would have seen you and your condition at the time. How do you think they view you as a mother today? If they had to choose you or Grant to be the custodial parent for Scotty, who would they pick?"

Alex noted the pained look that passed between his client and her father. It prompted him to explain, "Divorce is hard on the families and friends involved. Some want to back away from the situation because it intimidates and frightens them. Without meaning to, they treat you as if you're untouchables, leaving you feeling isolated."

He leaned forward, his elbows on his desk. "Others want to help because they love both of you and can't bear to see a breakup. So they downplay your problems in an attempt to get you reconciled, and that in turn makes you feel distanced from them because they seem so incapable of understanding the true situation.

"Generally speaking, however, most friends and relatives follow the course of human nature and take sides. Deep down they've had opinions and loyalties about both partners, which they may never have expressed aloud. Unfortunately, during a marital breakup, their true feelings surface."

Alex could see Tess shudder. She said, "I already know how Pastor Carr feels about me."

Lowell Carr's name was at the top of her list. It concerned Alex that Tess wouldn't be able to count on her clergyman for comfort during the traumatic days and months ahead.

"He officiated at Tess's marriage and christened Scotty," her father said. "I think it's unconscionable of the man to interfere in a situation that's out of his range of expertise. His job is to be a spiritual counselor to both Tess and Grant. Refusing to take the word of my wife and daughter when he has known them so many years is very disheartening."

"I couldn't agree more, Dr. Jenner."

Tess turned to her father. "Alex says it's possible the pastor might even testify against me."

"Are you serious?" Dr. Jenner asked in a tone of utter incredulity. The noted surgeon was obviously an ethical, upstanding, rare breed of gentleman who'd never dealt with types like Medor. The Jenner family would be in for many more unpleasant shocks from now until the judge rendered his verdict, Alex knew. He'd have his work cut out preparing them.

"Owing to opposing counsel's reputation in prior cases, I wouldn't rule anything out, no matter how outrageous. I warned Paul Wong that the box of fruit and nuts he had delivered to your daughter and Scotty has already sent up a red flag to Medor."

The doctor made a protesting sound. "Do you mean to tell me that Grant's attorney will try to prove that Tess encouraged the attentions of another man?"

"As I told your daughter, it's the way Medor does business. Because it's imperative that Tessa's integrity remain inviolate, Paul Wong won't attempt to communicate with her or Scotty until I tell him it's all right. That's why I want you to enjoy those leis while we talk, Tessa. They'll have to come off before you walk out of here.''

He watched as she touched the delicate orchids with her slender fingers. ''Now, having said that, I want you to forget Clive Medor and concentrate on telling me the whole truth and nothing but from beginning to end. That way I can prepare my case knowing there won't be any surprises.''

He pushed up his shirtsleeves and buzzed Burt to bring them some sodas. Without conscious thought his eyes shifted back to his client.

Helpless to do otherwise, he found himself admiring the classic cut of her black wool dress, the length of her well-shaped legs encased in sheer hose.

She must have felt his gaze because she looked up, catching him off guard. Her cheeks bloomed.

''Whenever you're ready,'' he prompted her in a husky voice not even he recognized.

HOWARD HAD JUST SAID goodbye to his last patient for the day when the receptionist told him Dr. Jenner was on the phone.

He picked up the receiver. ''Richard. Thanks for returning my call.''

''I'm sorry it's taken so long to get back to you about my daughter, but it's been one of those days.''

''For me, too. Knowing how busy you are, I wouldn't have disturbed you if I wasn't concerned about Tessa. She didn't come in for her appointment yesterday."

"I know. It's my fault. You see, I asked her to let me be the one to tell you the good news."

"Oh? What's that?"

"Over a period of time, I've discovered to my great joy that my daughter no longer suffers from depression. The condition brought on by the pregnancy has reversed itself at last. Before our family shouts it to the world, I have to tell you how grateful I am that, at the lowest ebb of her life, you were there to pull her through some very dark moments. I'll never forget. But now a miracle has occurred. Wilma and I thank God that part of her life can be put behind her."

"Well, Richard, if you're certain a miracle has occurred, then I couldn't be happier for Tessa. I wish her the very best."

"Thank you. I'll tell her that. Goodbye, and thank you again for everything."

Howard hung up the phone, slipped a Life Saver into his mouth and buzzed Elsa. "What time is that Colorado Psychiatric Association dinner at the Radisson tonight?"

"Seven-thirty. But the secretary phoned and said you're supposed to be there at seven, because you're president-elect and they're having a quick board meeting you need to sit in on."

He glanced at his watch. It was quarter to six. "I'm barely going to have time to finish up here and dash home to change clothes. Do me a favor and call

Sleepy Hollow Sanatorium. Tell the desk I'll be by to have lunch with Mother tomorrow.''

"Will do.''

He hung up and reached for Tessa Marsden's file:

February 9—Patient's father returned phone call with news she no longer suffers from depression and won't need my services any longer. The father could be in denial. More probable theory is that he's using his professional status to shield daughter from further exposure, thus preventing certain facts from coming to light: i.e., probable use of illegal drugs, possible pregnancy, liaison with man in Hawaii, long-term obsession to divorce husband.

Am fearful for life of patient and welfare of her son. Suspect her original manic-depressive condition has increased in severity. Will continue to stay in touch with patient's husband and be of assistance to his attorney.

"MOMMY?" SCOTTY CAME running when he heard her key in the lock. "How come you're so late?"

"I'm sorry, honey," she said as she swung open the door and stepped inside. "I've been apartment-hunting and think I've found one near the school you'll like."

Tess hung up her coat, then swept her son up into her arms.

"Why can't we stay here?"

"Because this is Nana and Grampa's home. We need one of our own. A lot of children live on the same block."

Besides that plus, the basement apartment of the older home had a cozy feeling and wasn't too expensive. The widow who lived upstairs seemed very pleasant.

"Are they in my class?"

"I don't know. We'll go over there next week when the apartment is vacant and check it out."

"Goody." He sniffed noisily. "Mommy, you smell like flowers."

Stunned by his uncanny observation, she stammered, "D-do I? I guess it's the perfume I'm wearing." Six hours had passed since she'd been in Alex Sommerfield's office, yet the oils from the orchid petals still clung to the front of her dress.

No matter how hard she tried, she couldn't forget the indescribable sensation of his hands touching her hair as he'd put the leis around her neck, the intensity in his brilliant blue eyes.

"Do you know what? I've missed you." She kissed her son's freckled nose. He in turn planted a wet kiss on her mouth.

"Mmm—" she rolled her eyes "—you taste like SpaghettiOs."

"How did you know what Nana fixed me?"

"Because I'm the smartest mommy in the world."

"Susie says you're the sickest mommy in the world. But you're all better now and don't have to take any more medicine, right?"

If someone had plunged a dagger in her heart, Tess couldn't have felt more pain. For Susie to make a remark like that, she must have heard it from her mother, Ruth, Grant's sister.

"That's right, Scotty," she said in a firm voice to camouflage the hurt. "I'm completely well. No more doctors, no more pills. Ever."

She lowered him to the floor. "When did you talk to Susie?"

"Today. Uncle Winn picked me up after school, and we took the stilts over to her house for her birthday."

Bless Winn for carrying through. "Did she like them?"

"No."

"Why not?"

"Because she kept falling down. I did, too. Uncle Winn tried to teach us how to walk, but Susie just got madder and madder and ran in her house crying."

"Oh, dear. How about you? Did you cry?"

"One time I did," he admitted. "Uncle Winn told me to keep trying and pretty soon I'd be able to walk everywhere on them."

"I'll help you practice in the morning."

"Can I take my stilts to our house when Daddy picks me up tomorrow night?"

Tess had forgotten all about Grant's midweek visitation, probably because she dreaded it so much she'd blocked it out of her mind.

"Of course," she replied, trying to inject some enthusiasm into her voice when she felt like screaming. "He'll be so proud of you he'll get out the video camera."

"Come with us, Mommy."

"I can't, honey. That's your special time with Daddy. I bet he's planning to take you shopping for valentines to give your friends at school."

She had no idea what Grant's plans were. But judging by the way Scotty's face lit up in reaction, it had been the right thing to say and provided the necessary distraction.

"Scotty, did Grampa eat dinner with you?"

"No. He's still at the hospital."

"Where's Nana?"

"On the phone with Aunt Rae."

Tess could hardly breathe wondering what Dr. Milhouse's reaction had been when her father talked to him—as he no doubt had by now. Well, she'd just have to wait.

"Since Nana's busy, why don't you take your bath and tell me what you did at school today."

They started up the stairs together.

"We got to use the poster paints. Misty Anne tipped hers over and Mrs. Janke got real mad."

"That doesn't sound like Mrs. Janke."

"She's going to have a baby. Misty Anne says it makes her cross. Mommy, are you going to have a baby?"

Now why would Scotty ask a question like that? "No," she said, and hurried him along to the sunny bedroom done in shades of yellow and white with its matching en suite bathroom. There were picture windows on two sides.

Heavy snowfall had made the wooded property a winter fairyland. Deer had wandered down from the mountains and set up residence. Tessa couldn't imagine a more delightful room for the two of them. It was the kind of place she and Scotty needed at this precarious time in their lives.

While she changed into a nightgown and robe, she heard Scotty say, "Are you sure?"

Tess blinked. "Am I sure about what, honey?"

He followed her into the bathroom where she turned on the bathtub faucet and helped him off with his clothes. "Susie said we're having a baby. That's why you were throwing up."

On that note he plopped into the water and reached for the soap. Tess got down on the tile floor and rested her arms on the rim of the tub, schooling herself not to react.

"Susie says a lot of things. I'm not having another baby, but it wouldn't surprise me if Aunt Ruth was. Ask your daddy tomorrow. He'll know. Now let's get that hair washed."

Minutes later Tess's father walked in amidst playful chatter and giggles. His smiling face was the first thing she saw when she looked over her shoulder.

He hunkered down beside her. While Scotty made engine noises and skimmed his rubber boat over the bathwater, Richard said in a confiding tone, "You can't argue with a miracle. Dr. Milhouse behaved in a totally professional manner at the news that you wouldn't be coming to him anymore. He wished you well."

"I'll bet he was furious."

"I suspect so, too," her father murmured, "but his hands were tied."

"Thank heaven."

"Forget him, sweetheart. It's all behind you now."

The relief was exquisite. Little by little Tess felt the tension leave her body. In fact she had about as much energy as a cooked noodle. It was in this condition that her mother came to the bathroom door. She motioned Tess to join her.

"I hate to break up this happy scene, but Grant's on the phone."

Tess's spirits plummeted. "He's probably calling to work out visitation for tomorrow night. Thanks, Mom. You're a saint." She kissed her mother's cheek, then stepped past her to enter the bedroom.

"Yes, Grant?" She sat down on the yellow-and-white-checked bedspread.

"What took you so long? Are you sick again?"

Alex had warned her to ignore any baiting, any goading, to remain calm and in control no matter what her husband said or did. "No, but thank you for asking."

"I'm planning to pick Scotty up from school tomorrow."

Her first instinct was to say no, because she wanted to feed him a snack before he went with his father. But voicing any objection would be playing into Grant's hands, something Alex had warned her never to do.

"That's fine. He wants you to see him walk on his new stilts. I'll send them to school with him. I think he's hoping you'll work with him on some valentines, too."

"Let's get something straight, Tess. You're in no condition or position to decide what I do or don't do with my son anymore. You'd better get used to it."

She froze in place because Grant sounded so hostile. "He's *our* son, Grant. I'm trying to help make his visits happy ones."

"I'm going to hold you to those words when he's living with me on a permanent basis."

Long after the line went dead, Tess's hands were still clutching the receiver in a death grip.

CHAPTER EIGHT

WHILE TESS WAITED in Scotty's classroom for Mrs.
Janke to come back from lunch, she inspected the
unique artwork displayed on the walls. Scotty grew
impatient for her to see his latest masterpiece and
pulled her down the far aisle.

"This is mine, Mommy." He pointed proudly.

Tess could have picked it out from all the others.
He had a definite flair for art and design, just like
Winn, and had painted a remarkable beach scene in
Hawaii with palm trees and seashells. But her smile
faded when she realized who the three figures in the
boat represented.

"That's you, that's me and that's Mr. Wong,"
Scotty said innocently. "Can I send it to him for a
present?"

A sick feeling in the pit of her stomach almost im-
mobilized Tess. If Grant got a look at this...

"Yes, honey. He'll love it. I'll tell your teacher I'm
going to take it home with me."

"Goody."

"Mrs. Marsden?"

Tess wheeled around. "Hello, Mrs. Janke."

"I thought I heard your voice."

"How are you?" Tess asked. "Scotty tells me you're expecting another baby."

"Yes, but not until June." Tess thought the teacher sounded tense and unusually abrupt.

She looked around for Scotty; he'd wandered out of earshot to the bird perch where Mrs. Janke's brightly plumed cockatoo walked back and forth making occasional squawking sounds.

"Mrs. Janke, I wanted to let you know that Scotty's father will be picking him up after school today."

"Yes. He's already informed me."

A shiver chased across Tess's skin. "I see." She tried to keep her voice level. "Then he's probably told you we're getting a divorce."

"Yes."

Tess stood there waiting for some word of commiseration or sympathy, if only for Scotty's sake. But there was none. The knife twisted a little deeper. Whatever Grant had said to Mrs. Janke had changed the relationship between the teacher and her. They'd never been friends, exactly, but they'd always been cordial with each other. Now Mrs. Janke seemed to be treating her as though she was lacking, somehow.

Tess took a deep breath. "This is going to be a traumatic time for Scotty. Please let me know if you're worried about him or notice anything unusual about his behavior. I'll come here and discuss it with you right away."

"It's too bad you didn't call first for a conference today. Lunch is almost over and I don't have time to get into a discussion about Scotty now."

An alarm went off in Tess's head. "Do we need to?"

"When there's trouble in the home, a child always shows signs. I've discussed them with your husband when he's felt you weren't up to it."

Dear God. How long had that been going on? Tess's stomach lurched, and she felt perspiration film her skin.

"Your husband told me you've been sick since your return from Hawaii, but apparently you're having a good day. I'm glad, because Scotty was anxious to show you his artwork."

She gestured at Scotty's picture. "He's very talented. But as I told your husband, this particular picture has more life than anything he's ever done. The man you met in Hawaii certainly made a big impression."

The sick feeling intensified. "I'd like to take it with me."

"I'm afraid your husband has already asked for it."

Tess had to fight to stay in control. "That's fine, just as long as Scotty gets it."

The school bell rang. "We'll have to continue this another time," Mrs. Janke said.

"I'll call the office and arrange it." Turning on her heel, Tess headed toward Scotty, who was standing with a bunch of children making the cockatoo talk. To their delight, it could say a dozen different things and held them all captivated.

She came to a standstill. Maybe it would be better if Scotty stayed distracted. She could leave now and he wouldn't notice.

After the meeting with Mrs. Janke, Tess was terrified to realize how little she knew about her husband's activities, how much had gone on behind her back. Grant had probably given the teacher input since Scotty's first day at kindergarten. It would explain why she and Mrs. Janke had never really gotten on. Under the circumstances, Tess didn't trust herself to say goodbye to her son without breaking down.

She needed Alex. At the door, she glanced back one more time at Scotty. He was still engrossed in the bird's antics, so without further hesitation, she hurried out of the building and climbed into her car.

Unmindful of the snow falling, she exceeded the speed limit to the high school where she worked. There was a phone in the faculty lounge she could use. She dashed inside and called his office.

"He's out of the office right now, Mrs. Marsden," she was told, "but give me a number where you can be reached and I'll make certain he calls you back."

Crushed because he wasn't there, Tess had no choice but to leave her home and work phone numbers with his paralegal. She knew he would inform

Alex as soon as he could, but that brought her little comfort.

Her body was surging in reaction to her conversation with Mrs. Janke. It was almost as if she was undergoing withdrawal all over again.

After asking the office to alert her if there was a message, she hurried upstairs to the choral room. At a time like this, she was thankful for the absorbing job of coaching the boys' barbershop quartet. It helped keep her terror at bay.

But once her work was over, the pain became excruciating. Not only was there no Scotty at her parents' home to greet her, she still hadn't heard from Alex.

She imagined that every one of his clients felt the same way about him, that he was the only person who could make sense out of chaos, this man who possessed the power to right a world spinning out of control.

How did he find a moment for himself? Did he ever get a good night's sleep when so many of his clients' lives hung in the balance.

ALEX LET HIMSELF in the back door of his law suite and made himself some coffee. Everyone in his firm had gone home for the day.

After a successful afternoon in court, followed by a game of handball with a colleague, he loved stripping down to his shirtsleeves. With a cup of hot coffee in hand, he moved through to his office to face the inevitable pile of messages.

From the doorway his gaze darted automatically to the message taped to his phone receiver.

Any one of a dozen current clients could be calling him about something vital or trivial. But deep in his gut he wanted it to be Tessa Marsden.

He was in trouble, he realized.

Every time he thought about her, which was a great deal more often than could be considered wise, he experienced an inexplicable excitement.

At first he deluded himself into thinking it was the bizarre nature of her case, the almost insane cruelty of the suit Clive Medor was building, that made him want to take her someplace far away and protect her.

But that was only a small part of it. There was something else going on at a fundamental, even primitive, level. Some chemistry he couldn't explain.

He could swear she felt the same way. The feeling persisted when he approached his desk and read the taped message.

"Call Mrs. Marsden ASAP."

To tamp down his emotions and armor himself against her powerful charisma, he purposely returned the other calls first, knowing fully well that hers should have taken top priority.

Alex grimaced at her nightmarish situation. He doubted a person on trial for murder could be suffering as much anguish as this woman who could very easily lose custody of her only child. But by the grace of God and his own hard work, Alex would move heaven and earth to prevent that from happening. He'd made her that promise and he intended to keep it.

TESS DID NOT FIND visitation getting any easier.

Every minute that Scotty was with Grant, she died a little more worrying about what was going on, what lies Grant could be planting in their son's mind to alienate him from her. There was always the fear that Scotty would call because he wanted to come home early and couldn't.

And there was another fear, the one she didn't want to talk or think about. The fear that Scotty would decide he'd rather live with his father and not come home at all.

To prevent herself from going out of her mind until Alex phoned—she prayed he'd phone—Tess hurried into the study and sat down at the grand piano. She needed to practice the accompaniment to the various songs the barbershop was singing for their performance. The medley spanned fifty years of music, starting with famous hits from the Second World War.

As she played "If I Could Be with You One Hour Tonight," an image of Alex in uniform haunted her thoughts. If a man like that had belonged to her, it would've killed her to see him go off to war.

Not until the piece was over did she realize how much he'd become an obsession. Maybe being forced to take medication all these years had affected her sanity. Imagine fantasizing about her divorce attorney! The mere idea was ludicrous, absurd. Shameful.

She stood up so abruptly she almost toppled the piano bench. Her parents had gone out to dinner with friends. They'd urged her to join them and stop worrying about Scotty for a few hours, but she'd declined.

Of course, they didn't know that on top of her concern over her son, she'd put in a call to Alex. It was another one of those impulsive panic phone calls, one her mother would suspect wasn't entirely necessary. She knew Tess's secret—that her daughter was more than a little attracted to her attorney.

Tess knew there was no point in fooling herself any longer. She found Alex Sommerfield unique among men, desirable in ways she didn't dare think about.

But until the divorce was final, she couldn't be seen dating anyone. Certainly not her attorney, even if he returned her feelings. Not only was it unethical, but her conscience wouldn't have allowed it.

Dear God, to be free to love a man like that, to be loved by him...

Her guilt was overwhelming. For she was still married to Grant, and years ago she'd sworn to love him until death. When she'd repeated those vows, she'd thought only of death in the accepted sense of the word.

It had never occurred to her that there could be another kind of a death, one more devastating in its way than the end of physical life. It was to be chained in an unhappy marriage—a living death. To stay with Grant would be perpetuating pain, hopelessness, despair, fear, sorrow. It meant creating new monsters, hacking away dreams, destroying goals, robbing pleasure. It meant condemning Scotty to a hell he didn't deserve or ask for.

She stood there in the study and buried her face in her hands. "Scotty," she whispered. "Forgive me, forgive your father for what we've done, what we're doing to you.

"Please, God, help me to do the right thing. Help me to stay strong, help me to keep my head on straight. And forgive me for having thoughts about Alex—"

Her prayer was interrupted by the ringing of the telephone. Weak and dry-mouthed, she crossed to the end table, picked up the receiver and said a shaky hello.

"Tess?"

The concern in his voice acted as a trigger. With so many conflicting emotions bubbling to the surface, she was reduced to tears. For a minute she couldn't say anything and sank onto the arm of the couch while she tried to get herself under control.

"I think we need to talk," Alex said. "How soon can you be at my office?"

"I—I'm not sure . . ." Her voice still shook. It was humiliating.

"If there's a problem about a sitter, I can come there."

"No!" She half groaned. What if Grant brought Scotty back while Alex was at the house? She could just imagine the construction her husband would put on that. Maybe in an emergency an attorney might go to the home of a client to do business. But Grant would never see it in that light.

"S-Scotty's on visitation tonight," she said to explain her outburst.

"Since your husband will probably bring him home at the latest possible moment, we should have plenty of time. It's only six-thirty. I'll expect you in my office at seven."

"That isn't fair to you."

"I live by a different timetable, Tess. What's important here is that we equip you for the fight ahead. If that means an evening conference, then fine."

So help her, she needed to see him. "I'm leaving now."

"I'll meet you downstairs to let you in the building. The streets are icy. Be careful."

"I will. Thank you."

In order to get downtown and back in time to be home for Scotty, Tess didn't bother to change out of her jeans and white turtleneck. After leaving a note on the front-hall table for her parents letting them know where she'd be, she grabbed her parka and purse, then dashed out to her car.

Since the sun had gone down, the temperature had dropped. Alex was right—the morning slush had turned to black ice, making the drive into the city treacherous. But with so much on her mind, she didn't really think about it. At last she pulled into a parking space across the street from his building.

She spotted Alex's tall powerful frame immediately. He must have seen her park because he stepped outside the doors of the ten-story office building, not having bothered with a coat or jacket. His shirt-sleeves were rolled up to the elbows and he'd removed his tie.

She started across the intersection. The closer she got to him, the faster her heart thudded. To see him standing there waiting for her was like coming home after being lost in a dark abyss for years and years. Never in her life had she experienced a feeling like it.

THE ELEVATOR WHISKED THEM to the sixth floor in a matter of seconds. In that short amount of time, Alex was bombarded by a dozen new feelings and sensations—none of which, he knew, would stand up under close scrutiny.

She stood several feet away, as tall as his chin, her gaze fixed on the doors. The light from the ceiling exaggerated the hollows in her cheeks, the shadows beneath her dark lashes. Most of all it brought out the luster of her rich brown hair, which she'd left loose. It hung almost to her slender waist from a side part.

In profile, she was exquisite, a goddess. And when those great eyes suddenly turned to him, full of pleading, he saw fire and passion in their golden brown depths. And anguish of soul.

Every instinct screamed for him to take her in his arms and comfort her in ways he had no right to be entertaining. Only by the greatest strength of will did he remain motionless until the doors opened at his floor.

Another attorney in the law firm stood waiting for the elevator. His gaze swung immediately to Tess Marsden.

She couldn't help filling the vision of any male who came within sight of her. Forty-year-old Mitch Gardner was no exception. He was married with three children, but it didn't stop him from checking her out, as she exited the elevator, in a way that made Alex's jaws clench.

He sensed the exact moment Mitch's speculative gaze flicked to him, but by that time the doors had closed.

Alex knew exactly what was going on in Mitch's mind. Right now the corporate attorney was wondering if the gorgeous creature in the elevator was Alex's client or Alex's girlfriend—or both. Such speculation was the reason Alex had never invited a female client to come to the office after business hours. Oh, well, too late now.

Tess removed her parka and walked into his office ahead of him. He had an idea she was oblivious to the reaction she'd caused out in the hall seconds ago. Oblivious, as well, to the reaction she caused in him. She had no idea that the way she looked in jeans and pullover took his breath away.

From the beginning he'd felt that she was a person who had no sense of her impact on the opposite sex. In Alex's eyes, that quality made her all the more attractive.

"Can I get you something to eat or drink before we start?" He realized his question came out rather brusquely, but he was trying to remain professional when it was the last thing he wanted to do.

"No. Nothing for me, thank you."

"If you don't mind, I'll pour myself some coffee."

Excusing himself, he strode into the kitchen and made instant in the microwave. One of the guys had left a half-eaten package of sweet rolls on the counter. Having given dinner a miss, he devoured two of the rolls while he waited.

When he returned to his office, he determined to separate himself emotionally from her and get down to business.

"So tell me what happened today. What's upset you?" he asked the second he was seated.

She took a deep breath. "I went to Scotty's class to talk to his teacher and found out that Grant has had this relationship with her I didn't know anything about.'' Her voice shook.

Alex listened while she poured her heart out. Nothing she revealed surprised him in the least. Tonight he had the unpleasant task of ripping the veils from her eyes until she understood what a custody suit was all about, particularly one that Clive Medor was orchestrating.

''Tess—'' he sat forward in his chair ''—listen to me. I'm not a psychiatrist and don't pretend to be. But based on everything you've told me, it's my opinion that your marriage was in trouble long before you gave birth to Scotty. Furthermore, I believe the depression you suffered after taking him home from the hospital would never have occurred, had you been able to obtain a divorce then.

''But because of your strong sense of duty, your child and your religion, you stayed with your husband. Thus you were trapped. With no way out, depressionlike symptoms set in. A condition that, in my opinion, was misunderstood and misdiagnosed by your psychiatrist.''

Alex saw her eyes shimmer with unshed tears. ''The fact that you've been able to go off the medication and feel perfectly normal,'' he went on, ''is proof you were never manic-depressive in the first place. What I find truly remarkable is that, in spite of a bad marriage, you've managed to raise a wonderful boy and finish up your degree at the university while under the influence of heavy medication you didn't need.''

He paused, then finished, "That is what I believe, and that is the case I am going to lay before the judge."

"Thank God you believe in me." Her voice caught. "You'll never know what your words mean to me."

Her heart-wrenching sincerity tugged at his deepest emotions. "I'm not the only one who believes in you, Tessa. Your parents, son, brother and sister-in-law, Paul Wong—they know the truth, too. We're all behind you a hundred percent."

Alex's eyes bored into hers. "It doesn't matter what Scotty's teacher thinks or says. It doesn't matter what *anyone* else thinks or says, because they don't know the whole truth. *You and I do.* Together, we will take control of this situation. Do you understand what I'm telling you?"

She stared at him for the longest time before she nodded.

"It's vital that you do," he said in a strong tone. "Clive Medor is boasting that this case is going to set a precedent for the state of Colorado. He intends to strip you naked, so to speak, to prove that your husband should have custody."

She blanched at his candor, but he had no other choice. Tessa Marsden was a babe in the woods. She needed coaching to get her through the next few months.

"Is . . . is there going to be a jury?"

Alex shook his head. "The judge will be your jury. His job is to listen to all the testimony and then de-

cide which parent Scotty should live with on a permanent basis. Lately the media has reported a trend
in fathers' getting custody, but believe me when I say
the court still favors the best parent. Judge Larkin will
be presiding. I've argued several cases before him.

"He's a tough intimidating judge, severe with witnesses and counsel alike. But I'm glad he's the one
hearing your case, because the decisions he's handed
down to date show remarkable wisdom. I'm counting on that wisdom to see through Medor's tactics no
matter how brilliant they are."

"*Is* my husband's attorney brilliant?"

"Yes," Alex said. *Brilliant, but also malevolent,
which makes him particularly dangerous where you're
concerned.* "He's the best at what he does."

She gave a tiny gasp. "You're warning me, aren't
you."

"Yes, I am. You need to know what you'll be facing."

"Tell me more," she demanded, sitting straighter
in her chair.

He nodded approvingly. "First of all, you and
Scotty are no longer free to leave the city without the
consent of the court. After the preliminary hearing,
where the judge will interview Scotty privately, you
and your husband and Scotty will be ordered to undergo a battery of psychological tests.

"Because of your history of manic-depression and
your husband's charge that you're on drugs, you'll
also be sent to a court-appointed psychiatrist. There'll

be a custody evaluation, which entails your going into group therapy. I have to warn you that all those tests will be hard on you if you're not prepared. That will be my job."

The blood drained from her face.

"When the results are in, a trial date will be set and witnesses pro and con will be subpoenaed. When the trial's over, the judge will weigh the evidence and render his verdict. Then the divorce will be granted."

Tess looked as if she was going to faint.

"Are you all right?" he asked, alarmed.

"I'm so frightened I feel ill."

"I know. Just remember one thing. You're not going to lose Scotty."

She clutched the edge of his desk until her knuckles turned white. "I want to believe you."

"Then believe me."

Her answer seemed a long time in coming. When she finally said, "I do," he expelled the breath he'd been holding.

In the stillness that followed, with only his desk lamp illuminating the darkness, he could easily imagine that they were the last two people on earth, connected by a bond more powerful than anything Alex had ever felt in his life.

Afraid of being tempted beyond his endurance, he stood up. "Come on. I'll walk you out to your car. We've both had a long day, and I know you want to be home to greet your son."

CHAPTER NINE

TESS GROANED when she saw Grant's Oldsmobile in front of her parents' house. Then she saw the headlights come on. Grant must be leaving, which meant Scotty was already in the house with her parents. Since she and Grant had nothing to say to each other, she hoped he'd ignore her and just drive of.

It was ten after nine, earlier than she'd expected him to bring Scotty back. Thank goodness she hadn't stayed at Alex's office any longer.

She would probably still be there if he hadn't brought their conference to an abrupt end. Over and above her nightmarish situation, she harbored the new fear that Alex could sense her strong attraction to him.

Given the extraordinary man he was, it was probably an occupational hazard. He'd probably learned how to circumvent unsolicited female attention by saying what he had to say, then ushering his women clients out of his office as fast as was humanly possible while still remaining cordial.

Tonight the man had been brutally honest about what lay ahead and had asked for her full cooperation so he could win this case. The last thing he needed was a woman who was acting like a lovesick teenager.

She switched off the ignition and jumped out of the car, still carrying the shame of having exposed this vulnerable, pathetic side of her nature to him. She vowed that from here on out she would never call him again unless it was a true emergency and she had no other recourse.

Her thoughts were so full of Alex she hadn't realized that Grant had gotten out of his car until he stood on the path leading up to the house, blocking her way.

Grant exuded hostility. "Where have you been?" In the freezing night air she could see his breath unfurl.

"On an errand." It was the truth.

His eyes narrowed in disbelief.

She wanted to ask him how his visit with Scotty had gone. But remembering how he'd snapped at her the last time, she refrained.

"Just so you know, I'm living with my folks for an indefinite period. Since you didn't want anything else out of the house, I've had everything put in storage and have found people to rent it. The phone was disconnected this afternoon."

Tess was so stunned by the news she could hardly think. Scotty no longer had a place he could truly call *his* home. She could have wept buckets.

"If you'd told me your plans," she said, "I would've come over and helped with the packing."

If I'd known what you were going to do, I would've stayed in the house for Scotty's sake and paid you rent from the money I'm making now.

"Oh, right. And have the men from the church—the guys who were helping me—watch you run into the bathroom every few minutes to be sick?" he asked scathingly.

Don't react, Tess. Just don't react.

"What about Scotty's things?" she asked in a quiet voice. All his pictures, books, stuffed animals and toys she'd left behind for him to enjoy until they moved to an apartment.

"Where else would they be but at my parents?"

She sighed. "If that's all, then let's say good-night. It's too cold to stand out here talking."

Apparently she'd said the wrong thing again because it unleashed a stream of invective.

"Damn you, Tessa. You've patronized me for the last time." His eyes glittered. "Damn you to hell!" he raged before stomping back to his car and driving off.

He'd used those exact words on their honeymoon when she refused to let him do things to her she wasn't comfortable with.

Now he was making her pay. The violently bitter man who wanted revenge was fighting to take Scotty away from her.

She buried her face in her hands, praying she hadn't waited until too much damage had been done to Scotty before she and Grant went their separate ways. Besides salvaging what was left of their own lives, they owed it to Scotty to give him the very best of themselves.

Tess dashed into the house, anxious to talk to Scotty. She wanted his warm loving body to cuddle. She needed to reassure him that everything was going to be all right.

"Honey? Is that you?" her mother called from the kitchen.

"Yes. Where's Scotty?"

"You dad's getting him ready for bed. Before you go up to join them, you need to call Alex. He phoned here a few minutes ago and it sounded important. I left his home phone number on the desk in the study."

Alex had called? They'd said goodbye at her car only forty-five minutes ago. The mere mention of his name had started her heart pounding.

Furious with herself for reacting like this, she headed for the study, willing herself to calm down. In all likelihood he'd forgotten to tell her something important, or maybe he'd heard from Grant's attorney and needed to advise her on a new development. It was also possible that Paul Wong might even be trying to relay a message. Whatever the reason for his call, it certainly couldn't be personal. She was crazy to think it was.

Crushed by her own logic, yet unbearably excited just to hear his voice again this soon after being with him, she picked up the receiver. With a trembling hand she punched in the number and waited.

He answered on the first ring, sounding different, on edge.

"Alex?" Her voice trembled. She sounded like the idiot she was. "Mom said you called. Is something wrong?"

"Not anymore."

His cryptic comment puzzled her. "I don't understand."

"As you're well aware, the streets were like an ice-skating rink tonight because the temperature dropped another ten degrees while we were in my office. I felt badly that our meeting had forced you to drive in such treacherous conditions."

Actually she hadn't noticed the conditions. She'd been too consumed by thoughts of him. His concern shouldn't have thrilled her, but it did. Too much.

"I-if anyone feels badly, I do, for calling you every time I'm upset about something."

"Well, now we're even because there was an ugly twenty-two-car pileup on the freeway ahead of me. There were several fatalities. I found myself looking for your car. To make matters worse, a semi right in front of me made a complete circle near the off-ramp, jackknifing into a couple of cars and almost hitting mine. I had visions of the same thing happening to you."

Tess's visions were equally horrific. He could've been killed! The thought was too devastating to contemplate.

"Thank heaven you're all right!" she blurted without thinking.

"That was my sentiment when I heard your voice. Now I can relax. No one should be out on a night like tonight."

It was incredible talking to him this way. She wanted it to go on and on. "I agree. But in our case I'm thankful you made time for me because I was able to put your excellent advice into practice even sooner than I expected."

"Oh?"

"Yes. My husband was here when I arrived. It could have been disastrous, but thanks to you, I didn't react."

"Tell me what happened."

By now Tess had removed her parka and was curled up in the love seat next to the desk. She spent the next few minutes telling him everything Grant had done. Little by little she broke down, confiding her pain about Scotty's no longer being able to go to their old home.

"Don't you know his home is where you are? Nothing else matters to a child."

He always knew what to say to comfort her. Moisture clung to her eyelashes. "You're right."

"I want to meet Scotty before the preliminary hearing. Can you bring him to my office on Friday at eleven? What I have to say to him won't take long. You'll be able to get him to school and go to your part-time job without problem."

She only had to wait a day and a half to see him again! Warmth flooded her body. "We'll be there."

"Good night, Tess."

"Good night," she whispered.

He always ended the conversation first. She put down the receiver, deep in thought. What would it be like to spend a whole day, a whole week, with Alex? To have him all to herself. No deadlines, no good-byes. What if they'd met under different circumstances? What if he'd been the man on the beach in Hawaii, instead of Paul Wong?

She stood up abruptly. This kind of thinking was dangerous.

"That must be quite a conversation you're having with yourself."

"Mom!" Tess's head jerked around.

"I'm surprised you remember who I am. Do you feel like talking about it?"

Hot prickles broke out on her face. "Talking about what?"

"Well, let me see. When your father and I went out this evening, we were under the impression you didn't want to leave the house. When we got home, we discovered that you'd gone downtown to meet with Alex. No sooner did Grant bring Scotty back than the phone rang and it was Alex urging you to phone him no matter how late the hour."

Tess sucked in her breath. "He was worried about me getting home safely."

"I can understand that. Your father and I missed having a bad accident by mere inches."

Tessa gasped. "Oh, Mom..."

"It's okay. Thank goodness everyone is home in one piece. Honey? What happened after your father and I left to go out to eat?"

Tess put her hands in her pockets, studying the design of the oriental rug. "After my talk with Mrs. Janke today, I pretty much fell apart. Grant has done untold damage. He's been doing it for ages. It's no wonder I don't have any kind of rapport with her."

"Why didn't you say something earlier? We would've stayed home and talked it over."

"Because I hate unloading on you all the time. It isn't fair. In panic, I phoned Alex's office from school, but he wasn't there. I left word for him to call me. That's the reason I didn't go to dinner with you."

"I knew something was wrong."

Tess nodded. "The thing is, by the time Alex called me back, I was so upset I could hardly say hello. He knew it. When he told me to come to his office, I didn't hesitate. I—I needed him, Mom."

A long pause ensued. "Apparently he did you a world of good."

"Yes. He opened my eyes to what's ahead. It's going to get much worse before it gets better. He told me to ignore what Grant or anyone else thinks or says. None of it matters because together, we're going to win this case. I trust him completely."

"That's pretty evident."

Tess stared at her mother. "He's wonderful, Mom. In fact, I can't find the words to describe him."

Wilma smiled. "Then don't try. From all accounts, he thinks you're wonderful, too."

Tess's heart hammered until it hurt. "I'd like to think so, but he's the kind of man who makes every client feel important. It's his job to defend the indefensible. Like Dad, Alex just happens to have this amazing bedside manner."

Her mother's brow quirked. "So what you're saying is that after a full day's work, Alex still has the time to invite anxiety-ridden clients to come to his office so he can comfort them? Then calls them on the phone for another half hour of conversation, just to make sure that they got home safely?"

"Mom . . ." Tess laughed nervously.

"Well?"

Tess bit her lip. "I—I'd give anything to meet a man like him some day."

"It seems to me you already have."

"You know what I mean."

"I'm not sure I do. Why don't you tell me?"

"He's a renowned attorney. I'm in the middle of a nasty custody battle with a medical history that terrified Milo Pett out of taking my case. And even if I *were* free—"

"He doesn't seem to be letting any of that bother him," her mom interrupted. "In fact I would never have associated the esteemed Alex Sommerfield with the anxious male voice calling to find out if you'd arrived home yet."

"Yes, but—"

"Tess, your marriage to Grant didn't work. It was a mistake that has been going on for more than six years now. Unfortunately it made you feel unworthy. And then to be diagnosed as manic-depressive . . ."

She shook her head. "If I see any sin you've committed, it's that you've been telling yourself you're unlovable, that you have no right to be loved or to reach out for love."

Her mother understood everything. "You're right, Mom. That's exactly how I've felt."

"So it's time to throw off the guilt. Forgive yourself and join the human race. I say hooray that you went to Alex's office tonight."

She walked over and hugged her daughter. "What you're feeling for him is normal, natural and healthy. Don't you see? This means you're coming back to life, honey. It's long past due." She smiled into her daughter's eyes. "Continue to listen to Alex and follow his lead. Keep your mind and your heart open to every new experience. You'll never know what the future has in store unless you embrace it."

Tess clung to her mother, thankful for those words, which relieved her of layers and layers of burden.

PINEVIEW REST HOME in Denver seemed a nice enough facility. But as Alex waited at the nursing station and watched the elderly in their wheel-

chairs—some dozing, others muttering senselessly—
he was thankful not for the first time that he'd been
able to afford round-the-clock nursing care at home
for his ailing grandparents.

At the age of ten, after he'd lost his parents in a car
crash, his paternal grandparents had stepped right in
to raise him. If he'd achieved any measure of success
today, it was because of them.

They'd only asked two things in return: to see Alex
with his own children and to die at home. He hadn't
been able to grant them their first wish. But because
of his lucrative law practice, he'd been able to make
certain they were expertly cared for in their own home
in Colorado Springs until they drew their last breaths.

His grandfather went first with a massive heart attack, then his grandmother with pneumonia six
months later. Alex and his wife had been at their
bedsides on both occasions. Thankfully, his grandparents had passed away before his divorce. At least
they'd been spared witnessing that.

"Mr. Sommerfield? We've located Mrs. Hatfield.
She's just had her dinner and is in the sun room
watching television. Right this way, please."

Alex followed the aide down the corridor, passing
more patients in wheelchairs and others who shuf-
fled along with their walkers. His throat swelled with
emotion. He was reminded so much of his grandparents in their declining days.

"Hi, Vivian. I've brought you a visitor."

"You have?"

"Hello, Mrs. Hatfield. I doubt you'll remember me. My name is Alex Sommerfield. Seven years ago, your daughter Stephanie came to me because she wanted a divorce. I was her attorney."

The gray-haired woman concentrated hard. Alex knew she wasn't as old as she looked or acted.

"No. I don't remember you." Tears filled her eyes. "Oh, but he was a mean one."

Alex knew she was referring to Stephanie's husband, an alcoholic and a wife beater. "The divorce changed her life. She's happy now." He sat down on a chair next to her.

Vivian rested her forehead in her hand. "I wish she'd come to see me."

"Your daughter tells me she comes every Sunday."

"I want to go home."

"I know."

Stephanie was a single mother now with too many responsibilities to allow her to also take care of her parent. Alex understood this, yet he felt great compassion for Vivian who, like his grandparents, wanted to be home in familiar surroundings.

"Vivian. I'm here to ask you some questions. They're very important. Will you try to answer them for me?"

She nodded.

"Do you remember your doctor? His name was Howard Milhouse."

Vivian blinked. "Yes."

Alex took a steadying breath. "Why did you go to Dr. Milhouse? What was wrong with you?"

"I don't know." She rubbed her forehead.

"Yes, you do. Think."

"I cried a lot. He hated it when I cried."

"Who hated it?"

"Melvin."

"Melvin was Stephanie's husband."

"Not anymore."

"No. Not anymore. Did Melvin send you to Dr. Milhouse?"

"I don't remember."

"Someone sent you."

"Stephanie didn't want me to cry anymore. That made him meaner."

"Why did you cry?"

"He kept hurting my baby."

"You mean Stephanie."

"Yes, my baby."

"Stephanie is happy now," he said again.

The old woman lifted her head and smiled at Alex. "I'm glad."

"So am I. Vivian, did you cry a lot when you were a little girl?" She shook her head. "When you were a teenager?" She shook her head again. "When did you start to cry?"

"When Melvin shoved my baby into the tub and turned on the hot water. I can still hear her screams." She put her hands to her ears.

Alex groaned. That was one incident Stephanie hadn't shared with him. "Melvin's in a place where he can't do that anymore." Thank God.

Getting to his feet, Alex grasped both her hands and squeezed them gently. "Thank you for talking to me, Vivian."

"You're welcome. Come see me again?"

"I will." He meant it.

Fortunately the temperature hadn't dipped as low as the night before. The highway seemed free of ice. Alex drove back to Colorado Springs without incident, his mind going over his conversation with Vivian.

In his line of work, Alex often ran on instinct. The elderly woman had displayed excellent recall, and instinct told him he could trust what she'd said. Contrary to Stephanie's fear that he'd probably make the trip to Denver in vain—as she'd expressed to him yesterday when he'd called to ask about seeing her mother—Alex was more than satisfied with the results.

An aide at the rest home corroborated Stephanie's assertion that the only medication Vivian received there was a mild sedative to help her sleep. Interesting, Alex thought, that her present doctor hadn't continued Dr. Milhouse's treatment for manic-depression. It was that very diagnosis that had barred Vivian from testifying at Stephanie's trial. Fortunately there'd been enough other witnesses to corroborate Stephanie's claims of abuse.

So had Vivian's manic-depression just magically disappeared by the time she'd been put in the rest home? Alex rubbed his jaw thoughtfully. Neither Vivian nor Tess had suffered depressionlike symptoms until a traumatic experience had sent them to the doctor.

Maybe Milhouse had misdiagnosed Vivian's condition, just as he had Tessa's.

And if he'd made a mistake with the two of them, maybe he'd made a mistake with other patients....

Burt had done a recent background check on Howard Milhouse. The man was well respected in the psychiatric community and would soon be serving as president of the state psychiatric association. Dr. Jenner had referred his own daughter to Milhouse on the recommendation of a colleague.

Still, Alex had had enough experience practicing law to know that a man's facade, no matter how spectacular, could hide a multitude of sins. For some strange reason, he couldn't shake the feeling that he'd stumbled on a mystery. Like all mysteries, it needed solving.

An hour later he walked in his condo and checked his answering machine for messages. When he heard Sadie's voice, no doubt wanting to invite him to another of her dinner parties, he suddenly saw a way to follow through on the hunch he'd had while driving home from Denver. He picked up the phone and punched in Sadie's number.

While he waited for her to answer, he attempted to deal with his disappointment that Tess hadn't tried to reach him at his office or at home today. It shouldn't have bothered him so much. In fourteen hours he'd be seeing her again. It wasn't such a long time to wait. To his chagrin, it felt like fourteen years. *Lord.* What was happening to him? He couldn't feel this way. He *mustn't.* He was her lawyer! And in his book a lawyer didn't get emotionally involved with a client. Not unless he wanted to commit professional suicide—and blow his client's case while he was at it.

"Sadie? It's Alex," he said as soon as she said hello.

"Counselor! I can't believe you called me back so soon. What a wonderful surprise. Normally I have to badger Burt to get you to return my calls. Is it true what I've heard? Have you been holding out on me?"

"What are you talking about?"

"Mitch Gardner and his wife sat at our table at the country-club dinner last night. He told us about this gorgeous creature he saw you with the other night."

Alex cursed silently.

"Shame on you for holding out on me. But I've decided to forgive you if you bring her to a little supper I'm having next week before the ballet."

"Mitch should get his facts straight before he minds other people's business," Alex said angrily. "I happened to be with a client who's fighting for her life right now."

There was a distinct pause. "Alex...I'm sorry. I didn't mean to offend you."

He loosened his tie with a jerk. "I didn't mean to come off sounding so harsh. Forgive me, especially when I'm going to ask a big favor of you."

"Finally! You know I'd do anything for you. What is it?"

"I need information of a very delicate nature."

"Sound as if you want me to spy for you or something. There's nothing I'd love more."

Alex chuckled in spite of the seriousness of the situation. "I know you do a lot of volunteer work at Mountaincrest Hospital."

"Yes, two days a week."

"Have you made friends with anyone in the admitting lab for outpatients?"

"Well...yes. I've been doing this job so long I think I'm friends with everyone."

"Good. Before I tell you what I need, I'll make you a promise that, if you're successful, I'll be your servant for life."

She laughed. "Boy, that's a rash statement. Especially coming from you." Then her voice sobered. "Alex, something really important must be going on."

His eyes closed. "It is. Trust me." In fact, it stunned him just how vital Tessa Marsden had become to him. "Here's what I want you to do..."

The conversation with Sadie lasted ten minutes, then he headed for bed. Unfortunately, since meeting Tessa, he'd had trouble sleeping. Tonight was no exception. By five in the morning, he gave up the battle and rolled out of bed and into the shower.

He was in his office by six, elbow-deep in work. An hour or so later he heard footsteps and lifted his head. "Is that you, Burt?" he called.

"I'm here." Burt breezed into the office. "I used to make it in before you. What's up?"

"I want you to arrange a couple of phone conferences. First, get in touch with Tessa Marsden's former obstetrician—he's at the Shady Brook Clinic. Then make contact with a Dr. Barnes at Pineview Rest Home in Denver. Here are their names and phone numbers."

Burt took the paper from him. "I'll get right on it."

"Mrs. Marsden and her son will be in at eleven." He reached for his wallet and handed Burt a twenty-dollar bill. "As soon as they arrive, run around the corner to McDonald's and bring us all some lunch. Get Scotty a Happy Meal. No cheese or pickles. Ask for root beer."

"Okay. In case you haven't had a chance to read the message I left, there's been a postponement in the Larsen hearing. Opposing counsel will reschedule."

"Good. I could use some uninterrupted time this afternoon."

"You've got it."

As soon as he left, Alex opened the Penman file and worked nonstop until Burt buzzed him.

"Boss? Dr. Barnes isn't in his office yet, but he normally returns calls after two o'clock. I told his receptionist it was important, so she'll make sure you're the first one he calls back."

"Good work."

"Dr. Williams is another matter. He's been out of the country for the past two years and won't be home for another year."

Alex frowned. "Where is he?"

"South Africa."

"Doing medical work of some kind?"

"No. According to his son, who's living in his house, the doctor and his wife are on a mission for the Church of Jesus Christ of Latter-day Saints."

"That's interesting. Can you get a number?"

"I've already got it. There's a nine-hour time difference, so that means it's five in the afternoon in Durban. If I should be able to get him on the phone now, do you want to talk to him, or shall I set up another time more convenient for you?"

"Now, by all means."

"Okay."

CHAPTER TEN

"MY TUMMY FEELS funny."

So does mine, thought Tess, smiling sympathetically at her son. The anticipation of seeing Alex had robbed her of an appetite. "It's because this elevator moves so fast."

When it stopped on the sixth floor, Scotty grabbed her leg and clung until the doors opened. "Where are we going?"

"To see a friend." She reached for his cold little hand and started down the hall. "See the words on the door? Mr. Alex Sommerfield."

Burt stood up the moment he saw them enter the suite. "Hello, Mrs. Marsden. Hello, Scott."

Tess greeted him, then removed both their wraps and put them on the brass coatrack near the door.

"How did you know my name?"

"Your mother told me you were coming today."

He craned his head. "Are you Alex?"

"No. *I* am," came the familiar low voice Tess craved hearing. With her heart in her throat, she turned her head and found herself trapped by a pair of ocean-blue eyes. For a moment she was staggered by the striking picture he made in a white shirt and charcoal gray business suit.

She finally tore her gaze from his before she revealed too much of her excitement. "Scotty, this is Mr. Sommerfield, the man who's helping me."

"Hello," Scotty said in a voice tinged with a mixture of fear and awe.

Alex moved closer and got down on his haunches. "Hi, Scotty. Your mother's told me so much about you I feel like we're good friends already. Will you call me Alex?"

"Okay."

"Good. Are you hungry?"

Scotty looked up at Tess, his face a study in concern. "Are we, Mommy?"

Alex burst out laughing. "Well, Mommy—" Alex winked at her and stood up "—I think we have our answer. Let's go in here where there's a dining-room table."

The two of them followed him into his conference room. Scotty's eyes widened. "That's the biggest table I ever saw!"

Tess felt Alex's chuckle work its way under her skin and stay there. "Well, we men have to have a big place to sit down and eat. Don't you agree?"

"Yeah." Scotty grinned.

"You grab a chair at the end of the table there, while I help your mother."

She knew it was unintentional, but Alex's fingers brushed the shoulders of her navy suit jacket as he urged her chair forward. Like licks of fire, his touch quickened her body.

Oblivious, Scotty sat down, with his mother on one side and then Alex on the other. Positioned as they were at the end of the oval table, they were able to look and talk to each other without strain.

"Do you know why your mommy brought you here today?" Alex asked the boy.

Scotty nodded. "She said you were going to talk to me about court."

"Actually, I asked her to bring you here so we could have lunch and you could ask *me* questions."

"You did?" Scotty looked delighted at the idea. She could have hugged Alex on the spot. He knew exactly how to put her son at ease.

Alex nodded. "If I were you, I know I'd have a whole bunch of things to ask."

After a slight hesitation, "What's court?"

"A place where your mommy and daddy are going to get their divorce. It's a room in a building not far from this one. A man, who's called a judge, is going to talk to them. He's sorry they've been unhappy and hopes the divorce will make them feel better. Then he signs the paper, and it's over."

"Oh. Is the judge scary?"

"A little. He has to walk with a cane because he hurt his leg in the Vietnam War. I think the pain makes him cross sometimes."

"Oh," Scotty said again, and his voice had a small tremor. "Does he like kids?"

"I'm sure he does. Whenever I see them come out of his room, they're licking a sucker."

"I like suckers."

"So do I. Do you have any other questions?"

"What if I have to go to the bathroom?"

"He has his own bathroom in his office. He only lets you little kids use it. We big guys have to go down the hall."

"Can Mommy and Daddy come in with me?"

"No. They'll wait right outside the door."

"Why can't they come in?"

"Because the judge thinks that children are smarter than their parents. He says parents drive him crazy because they do all the talking. The judge doesn't want to listen to them. He wants to hear what *you* have to say."

"When my daddy comes to school, Mrs. Janke tells me to go play."

Tess sought Alex's glance and they exchanged a silent message.

"That won't happen with the judge. He'll tell your parents to go take a hike."

Scotty giggled. "You're funny."

Tess's heart swelled. Alex showed more wisdom and common sense than any child psychologist. By giving her son an opening, Scotty was able to ask things Tess had had no idea were on his mind. Like magic, Alex continued to alleviate each little fear.

"McDonald's has arrived," announced Alex's paralegal. He handed each of them a sack and a drink.

"Yum. Mommy, he got me a Happy Meal! Thanks!" Scotty tucked right in to his food.

"Thank you," she said to both men, but her gaze lingered on Alex, trying to express her gratitude. His eyes danced over the rim of his root beer in response. She felt as if the sun had come out. Warm glorious sunshine after years and years of cold bitter darkness.

Suddenly she was ravenous. Her appetite had made a startling recovery. She devoured her hamburger and fries as quickly as Scotty did. By the time she'd finished, Alex had answered at least a dozen more of Scotty's questions with the diplomacy of a master teacher.

"Mommy?" Her son turned his big hazel eyes on her.

Tess wiped her mouth with a napkin. "Yes?"

"Do I have to go to school today?"

"Of course."

"But I want to stay here with Alex."

So do I, sweetheart. "I'm afraid Alex is a busy man who probably has to go to court today for someone else."

Scotty's blond head swiveled to the man on his left. "Do you?"

"I'm afraid so. But tell you what—after you and your mommy leave court next week, I'll take you around the corner to Sol's Deli. They make the best cheesecake in Colorado Springs. Have you ever eaten cheesecake?"

"Yes. My mommy makes it. I love it."

Alex's eyes flicked to Tess. They held a devilish gleam. "Is that right?"

"Come to Nana's house," Scotty said, "and Mommy'll make you some!"

Heat suffused her face. She looked away from Alex in guilty confusion. "It's time to go, Scotty, or we'll both be late for school." She spoke in his ear. "Put your sack and cup in the waste basket, then thank Alex for everything."

While Tess got up from the table, Scotty gathered up all the sacks and cups. When he'd deposited them, he walked over to Alex. "Thanks for inviting me here. Thanks for lunch."

"You're welcome." In a huskier tone he murmured, "Your mom is very lucky to have a son like you. See you next week."

Alex tousled Scotty's hair before escorting both of them through the suite to the reception area. Once there, he helped Scotty on with his parka.

"Tess?" Alex focused his gaze on her, as if studying every feature. It left her feeling breathless. After assisting her into her coat he whispered, "He's one terrific boy. We both know why. The judge is going to know why, too." He squeezed her upper arms gently, then released her.

Her body throbbed from the brief pressure of his hands long after she and Scotty had ridden the elevator to the lobby.

She moaned, almost wishing he'd never touched her. Now she'd spend every night tossing and turning, wondering whether he'd merely made an unconscious gesture or been overcome by the same desires driving her.

"Mommy? Are you sick again?"

"No, sweetheart. It's freezing out. I can't seem to get warm." She hoped lightning wouldn't strike her for telling Scotty such a blatant lie.

For she *was* sick in a way. But how could she tell Scotty that the cause and cure for her illness lay with the man they'd just left?

ALEX STOOD THERE in the reception area long after saying goodbye to Scotty and Tess. Every time she walked away, it got harder to let her go. He'd made another mistake just now.

He hadn't intended to do anything more than help her on with her coat. But at the last second, he was overcome with a need to touch her. He'd broken his own cardinal rule and feared it was only a matter of time before he broke more.

Now Scotty had entered the picture. A cute little guy Alex would've loved to let hang around his office. Judge Larkin would be enchanted by him.

"Alex?"

Jerked from his tortured thoughts, Alex spun around to see Gus, his law clerk. "Yeah, what's up? What have you got for me?"

"On Monday you told me to run a computer check on a Grant Marsden while I was over at Court Records doing some research on the Penman case."

Alex nodded, instantly alert. "And?"

"Well, nothing came up on the screen. On a whim I checked the microfilm and found out there was a file on a Grant Marsden at the state archives."

The state archives?

"It came in this morning. Have a look."

His eyes zeroed in on the front of the legal-size folder. Two names appeared. Grant Ellsworth Marsden and Tessa Cosgriff Jenner Marsden. The date leapt out at him. Six years ago.

With a feeling of dread, Alex opened the file. It was a standard two-page complaint for divorce brought by Grant Marsden, plaintiff, against Tessa Jenner, defendant, for incompatibility. The only property to be divided were the cars and furnishings that each had brought to the marriage. Brett Wilcox, an attorney with a local firm, had signed the document, which was dated March 16.

Stunned, Alex scanned the next sheet in the file. It was another document submitted for dismissal of the afore-filed complaint. It had been signed April 24, five weeks later. For some reason, her husband had changed his mind about divorcing her.

There was no copy of the summons. That meant Tessa had never received papers. But surely Grant had expressed his intentions to her. And if so, why hadn't she told him, Alex, about it?

He raked a hand through his hair. Had she held back this information because she was afraid it could be damaging to her case?

He was damn sure Medor knew about it and would wipe the floor with it and Alex in the courtroom. A shudder passed through him. He felt as if he'd just been poleaxed and thrown over a battlement to his death.

"Alex?" Gus eyed him with concern. "You've gone pale. Is this bad?"

Alex sucked in a breath. "That depends," he muttered icily. "By the end of the day, I'll know one way or the other. Gus?" He clapped the younger man on the shoulder. "Acting on a whim is what makes or breaks a case. You keep this up and you're going to rise to the top."

"If that happens, it'll be because of you."

"How so?" Alex shrugged into his overcoat.

"Because I wouldn't have thought to run that computer check in the first place. I didn't see the point."

Medor is counting on that. "The point is, Gus, you did it, anyway, then took it a step further and found something crucially important. Thanks."

Five minutes later Alex pulled out of the car park and merged with the traffic. Before he confronted

Tess, he needed to talk to Dr. Jenner and would take his chances that the busy doctor could fit him in. This couldn't wait.

THE REHEARSAL for the concert had run late. Tess worried that Scotty would be upset when she wasn't at school right on time to pick him up. Throwing on her parka, she hurried down the three flights of steps and ran out of the school toward the parking lot.

In the distance she saw a tall man standing next to a black Mercedes parked beside her car. She instantly thought of Alex . . . but no, it couldn't be. She must be hallucinating.

She wasn't.

"Alex!" She hurried toward him. Why was he here? Why did he look so . . . different? Had something happened to Scotty?

"Scotty's fine," he said, as if reading her mind. "Your mother's picking him up."

Though relieved at his words, her initial fear didn't lessen. Alex wasn't the same man who'd been reluctant to let her leave his office four hours ago. This man's cold expression would have sent Scotty running in the opposite direction.

Alex stared her down. "Do you know the Hermitage Restaurant?" he asked without preamble.

Something was wrong. Horribly wrong.

"Yes." Her voice shook. A French family ran the quaint *auberge* located on the outskirts of the city. He couldn't have chosen a better place for privacy.

"I'll follow you there."

Always the gentleman, he held her car door open while she climbed into the driver's seat, then closed it and walked to his own car.

The twenty-minute ride was a new dimension of agony for Tess. The man she could see in her rear-view mirror was a stranger.

She'd thought she knew him. She'd thought she knew his essence. Knew it from the first.

She felt a sickening sense of déjà vu. At one time she'd thought she knew Grant, but he'd turned into a stranger overnight.

Did one person ever really know another, or was she one of those people cursed with bad judgment?

None of her friends seemed to have the same problem. Sandra, Gwen, Janna—they were all happily married to wonderful men. And look at her parents, and Winn and Rae. They were happy, too.

Which meant there was something wrong with her, Tessa. For some reason, she didn't seem destined to find happiness. Maybe one of the boys she dated before Grant would have made her happy and vice versa, but she hadn't been attracted to any of them enough to consider marriage.

As for Grant, her attraction for him died on their honeymoon. Her desire had been completely destroyed.

No! That simply wasn't true. Her desire for Grant had been destroyed, but the desire she felt for Alex had her on fire.

These sexual feelings, mixed up with her admiration and respect for the man trailing her now, bore little resemblance to the feelings of the old Tess.

Had her mind made Alex into a hero? Is that what she was destined to do with every man who had the potential to be important to her? Had she granted Alex virtues he didn't possess? Could she really have been so blind where he was concerned?

Heartsick, she pulled off the highway into the parking lot of the Hermitage, the Mercedes right behind her. Bad weather must have been keeping patrons away because the lot was almost empty. Alex was out of his car and opening her door for her even as she reached for the handle. Without a word, he cupped her elbow and ushered her inside, then led her to a booth in the corner. When he tried to relieve her of her coat, she held on to it and slid along the bench, away from him.

Alex sat down opposite her. "What would you like to drink?"

"Nothing." She was on the verge of being sick to her stomach. Any minute now and she'd have to run to the washroom.

The implacable expression on his face seemed to harden before he asked for coffee from the man tending bar. Once the steaming brew had been placed on the table, Alex sat forward and impaled her with his gaze.

"Tess, if you've deliberately held back some vital information from me, I need to know now, because I won't represent a client who's lied to me or kept anything from me. I told your father as much before I drove over to your school."

Tess hadn't known what was coming, but his declaration knocked the foundations out from under her. She hadn't thought Grant's lies about her could touch Alex, not after everything they'd discussed.

How could she have been so wrong?

Like Milo Pett and Roger Thorn, Alex had weighed the odds and decided he couldn't win. He'd already told her father. *Dear God. I'm going to lose Scotty!*

The judge with the cane was going to weigh the evidence and give Scotty to Grant. That precious little boy she'd given birth to. The child of her body, her heart and her soul. The judge, a stranger who had total control over her life, would prevent her from raising her own son to adulthood. She couldn't stand it.

"Excuse me..."

She dashed to the ladies' room and reached the toilet just in time to lose her lunch. Then she rinsed her mouth and clung to the sink with both hands until her legs stopped shaking.

"Tess?" Alex had come right into the washroom.

She turned to him with watery eyes. "Maybe I'm the monster my husband says I am. But I'm not on drugs, even if you think I am. I'm not pregnant, even though my sister-in-law is telling the whole world I'm carrying Paul Wong's child. At this point I have no idea what my son is going to say to the judge. Who wants a sick mommy?''

She stared at the tiled floor, unable to look at Alex. ''For all I know, he can't wait to live with Grant,'' she mumbled, hardly coherent. ''None of it matters anymore. I've lost him, so there's nothing more to say. I'm sorry I wasted your time. Please send the bill to the house. My father will pay it. Poor Daddy.'' She shook her head. ''His little cross to bear.''

''Stop it, Tessa!''

''Go back to your *sane* clients, Mr. Sommerfield,'' she said in a frigid voice.

''I can't do that until I have some answers!''

In the next instant, he pulled her toward him. When she tried to break free, he pressed her head against his shoulder and clamped her hard against his body. His strength was too great. She went limp in his arms, depleted by a violent storm of sobbing.

When the first wave of tears had subsided, he demanded, ''Did Grant ask you for a divorce as early as three months into your marriage?''

''What? No, of course not!'' She raised her head from the sopping-wet material of his suit jacket. ''The last thing he wanted was a divorce. His pride couldn't have taken it. Why are you asking me this now?''

Like her shock over the question Dr. Milhouse had asked her about meeting another man, she thought Alex knew her better than that. She'd have sworn he trusted her implicitly. His question caused her unbearable agony.

"Do you swear before God you're telling me the truth, Tess?" He held her by the shoulders now and was actually shaking her.

"Yes. I swear it. I wouldn't dare lie in front of God. He's the only friend I have left."

"No. He's not."

CHAPTER ELEVEN

"WHAT ARE YOU SAYING?" She pulled away from Alex in shock. She was too frightened and heartbroken to make sense of anything.

"Tess—" he stood there with his hands curled into fists, his chest heaving "—we have to talk. I'll be waiting for you at the booth."

He strode out, leaving her staring at her chalk white face in the mirror.

Had Alex really run into the ladies' room after her? Crushed her in his arms until he got the answer he wanted, uncaring of who might walk in on them?

She had no idea what to make of that behavior or the things he'd said. She was absolutely bewildered. If another woman hadn't come in to the washroom just then, she didn't know how long she would've stood there, dazed.

She wished she had a toothbrush. Oh, well, she'd have to make do with another rinse. After washing her face, she brushed her hair and applied fresh lipstick.

Nothing could change the damage done to her on the inside. But she supposed that outwardly she looked presentable.

At her approach, Alex stepped away from the bar and brought her a drink.

"Some ginger ale. Maybe it'll settle your stomach."

Once again they were facing each other, but she couldn't look at him. She took a sip of her drink. It tasted good and so she swallowed a little more.

"After you left my office," Alex said after a moment, "Gus, my clerk, handed me a copy of a legal document he'd found doing research for me on your husband. It was a petition for divorce Grant filed three months after you were married."

Tess gaped at him. *"What?"*

Alex nodded grimly. "He never had it served. A month later it was dismissed."

"You must be mistaken."

"No."

She put her fingers to her temples. "Grant actually went to an attorney and filed for divorce? On what grounds?"

"Incompatibility."

An incredulous laugh escaped her. "I don't believe it. I mean, I do believe it, but I don't. Oh, I know I'm not making any sense."

"You're making perfect sense. Does the name Brett Wilcox ring a bell?"

She blinked. "Yes. He was Lyle's older brother. Lyle and Grant were best friends through high school and college."

"Apparently your husband went to Brett for legal counsel. He was the attorney of record."

Tess put her glass down so hard some of the liquid splashed onto the table. "Grant went to Lyle's brother about me?" She gasped. "Why didn't he tell me? I wanted one, too. I would've given it to him, no questions asked. He never said a word. I never dreamed—"

"Tess," Alex interjected, "Clive Medor will use this to prove you caused your husband grief *before* you became pregnant with Scotty. I've no doubt he'll try to tie in your inability to make the marriage work with the fact that you may have suffered from manic-depression all your life. He'll argue that you make a poor prospect for a mother."

As she stared at Alex, it began to dawn on her what he was saying. "No wonder you came to find me. You thought I'd deliberately withheld this information. It could cost you the case! Alex, you have to believe me. I would *never* have done that."

"I know that now. Don't you think I wanted to believe you?" The cords stood out in his neck. "Why do you think I went to your father first? He was as stunned as you are. But he agreed you might have kept that kind of news quiet from him and your mother because you found it too humiliating."

"I probably would have at first. To be married only three months and then have your husband wanting to end it would have been hard to admit. But if he'd asked, I think I would have welcomed it, and eventually I would have told my parents.''

''No one wants to believe their marriage has broken down.''

She heard undercurrents in his tone. He'd been through a divorce himself, so he understood.

''No. But I'd have been the last person to fight him. Deep in my heart I didn't want to stay with him.'' She smoothed the hair away from her face. ''This is a new nightmare. I didn't think things could get worse, but I was wrong. Alex, I'll understand if you don't want to represent me any longer.''

''Don't talk nonsense!'' he thundered. ''Now that I know of its existence, that document will end up hurting your husband, not you. Tess, the only two cases I ever lost against Medor were when my clients lied to me about something crucial. He's never let me forget.''

Alex leaned forward and spoke confidentially. ''I'm going to tell you something I shouldn't. It's my personal opinion that Medor has a vendetta against women. He gets far too much enjoyment out of telling me you don't have a prayer. To be blunt, he's a sick guy.''

Tess shivered. ''I feel the same way about Dr. Milhouse.''

He nodded. ''I apologize for coming on so strong with you. But this case is important to me. You're one person I won't allow those men to destroy.'' It sounded like an avowal.

I wasn't wrong about Alex, after all, she thought.
*He's everything I believed him to be and much, much
more.*

He walked her to her car. "I'm going to be out of
the office for three or four days, but I'll be back in
time for the pretrial next Thursday. If you need me,
call Burt. He'll know how to reach me."

"Will you be out of town?" She tried to hide her
disappointment.

"Yes."

She wanted to ask him if it was business or pleasure, but she didn't dare. She wanted to tell him to be
careful, to please come back safely, but she couldn't.
She wanted to ask him to phone her, any time of the
day or night. Impossible.

Before she did something she'd regret, like beg him
to take her with him, she got in her car and started the
engine. Forcing her gaze away from him, she drove
off. Each time she left him, the ache intensified.

ANOTHER DRAB WINTER afternoon in Denver didn't
prevent Alex from picking out the yellow Saab dart-
ing in and out of traffic toward him. With luggage in
hand, he strode past the droves of people coming and
going from the airline terminal.

When Sadie drew abreast of him, he tossed his bags
into the trunk of her car and climbed into the pas-
senger side.

"Welcome home from South Africa, Counselor."

"Thanks for meeting me, Sadie."

"My pleasure. Did you have a good trip?"

"A *good* trip?" he muttered, rubbing his eyes. In terms of getting a deposition from the doctor, yes. But he felt as if he'd lived his entire life inside a 747. Couple that with the complications Tess Marsden had created in his life and his answer was an emphatic, "No."

"Poor baby. A successful one, then?" She maneuvered through the traffic with ease.

He cursed. "Don't play games with me, Sadie. I'm too exhausted. Tell me what you've found. When Burt phoned me in Durban with the news, I couldn't get back soon enough."

"I had so much fun I've decided I want to be put on your payroll. Unofficially of course. Ralph wouldn't like it if he knew the lengths I've gone to for you. Maybe I was a private detective in a former life."

She was making light of this, but he had a gut feeling she'd put herself in jeopardy trying to help him out. "You're too good a friend. I should never have gotten you involved in this," he murmured.

"Relax, Counselor. I didn't do anything that anyone in the hospital who knows how to get into the computer can't do, and that's virtually everybody. Part of my job as a volunteer is to be able to use it when I'm assigned to various departments throughout the year."

Alex flashed her a tired smile. "All right. Out with it."

Her answering grin was positively devilish. "I hit the jackpot. It's all there on the back seat."

"*Now* she tells me."

The adrenaline kicked in as he reached around for the manila folder and began devouring its contents.

By the time she'd pulled up in front of his condo in Colorado Springs, he'd memorized the incriminating information and mapped out his strategy.

"The printout from the pharmacy was pure inspiration. Sadie, my love, I'd give you a medal if I had one. For the time being, this will have to do."

He leaned across the seat and gave her a long-overdue hug. She'd always been a true friend, a very precious commodity. "You've performed a miracle. One day I'll think of a way to repay you."

But even as he spoke, his mind was racing ahead. He wished he had the ability to clone himself. Everything had to be put in motion before Tess's case went to trial in a couple of months.

Sadie was chuckling and he looked at her in confusion before he got out of the car. "You told me you'd be my servant for life, as I recall," she said. "But I won't hold you to that if you'll let me meet her. That would be payment enough."

He frowned. "What are you talking about?"

One brow lifted. "You're a closed book, Counselor, but you and I go back to childhood and I can read you better than you think. Whoever she is, she's accomplished something no other woman has ever done, not even Betsy."

"Is that so."

She cocked her head. "Tell me why it is you couldn't send Gus or Steve to South Africa to do your legwork? It's not at all like you to put all your other cases on hold for a minor deposition."

After a brief pause, "Because I don't dare leave anything to chance where Tessa's life is concerned."

Sadie grinned. "If you could see your eyes..." She revved the engine. "You know the old cliché. Mirrors of the soul and all that. God bless, Alex."

After she drove off, he hurried into the building to the third-floor condo he'd lived in with Betsy. Its short distance to the downtown area, plus easy access to the freeway, had sold them on it.

After their divorce, he should've found himself another place, if only to create new memories. But he'd been in the middle of a couple of big cases at the time and had never gotten around to calling a Realtor.

That was two years ago. Lately he'd had no free time and no inclination to go through the process of a move. In Alex's mind, a traditional home was synonymous with a woman. His heart gave a lurch. If Tessa could be the woman waiting for him every night...

Hungry for her, even just the sound of her voice, he quickly let himself into his apartment. Before he did anything else, he checked his answering machine. There'd been a flood of calls from his staff, plus personal calls.

Nothing from Tess.

Tomorrow was Wednesday. Thursday was her pre-trial. A formality that would take twenty-five, thirty minutes, no more. And afterward, he was counting on Scotty's remembering his promise of a little trip to Sol's Deli, a gathering place for attorneys and clients alike. During the workweek, no colleague would question his being there with Tess and her son. Sol's was the closest place to the courthouse to grab a bite to eat. *A safe place.*

Ridding himself of his clothes, he got in the shower and turned on the cold tap full force.

As Scotty started to climb out of the back seat, Tess leaned over and kissed her brother's cheek. "Thanks again for bringing us to the courthouse. I'll call you when it's over."

Winn gave her another hug. "We'll all be home waiting. Are you sure you don't want me in there for moral support?"

"I'm sure. Alex said it would look better if I came on my own with Scotty, present myself as a confident woman and mother."

"You've achieved your goal." He took in her hair, which was arranged in a French twist, then the snowy white blouse beneath the tailored, dark brown suede suit. "It's no secret that my little sister has always been a raving beauty," he said with a curious tremor in his voice. "But today, despite what you're going through, there's a new subtle radiance about you.

Rae's noticed it too. When Grant sees you—" his voice hardened "—he'll be struck dumb by the change. It should make him think twice about the pointless torment he's subjecting you and Scotty to."

"Mommy! There's Alex!"

Her heart turned over. "I've got to go. Thank you for those kind words, dear brother. I love you." She pressed her cheek to his before getting out of the car.

Scotty hadn't waited for her. By the time Winn drove off, her son, dressed in his little navy church suit and tie, was almost to the top of the stairs leading into the courthouse. Tess dashed up the steps after him.

With all fears about visiting the judge disposed of, Scotty was eager to see Alex again. Since Friday he'd talked nonstop about him to her parents.

Tess was guilty of the same sin; she just hadn't said the words out loud. Now, after a seemingly endless wait, there he was in front of the doors, larger than life.

His taupe suit looked expensive and hand-tailored. She swallowed hard at the way it molded his powerful physique. When she dared meet his unswerving gaze, the moment held too much significance for her. No words would come out. Talk about being struck dumb.

"You look perfect," was all he said. His voice was husky.

Scotty reached for her hand. "Are we gonna see the judge now, Mommy?"

"Yes, darling."

She was still trying to recover from the compliment Alex had paid her. If he was giving her his seal of approval as attorney to a client, she was pleased. But she hoped, oh, how she hoped, it was more than that.

"Tess," he murmured beyond Scotty's hearing, "ignore what you see when you enter the courtroom. Let's go. I'll show you where to sit."

The ever-lurking nausea in the pit of her stomach came back with a vengeance. Scotty walked between the two of them as they entered the courthouse and passed through the security check.

"Judge Larkin's court is on this floor. Right around the corner. Do you want to open the door for us, Scotty?"

Thank heaven Alex had warned her. In one covert glance Tess saw a huge group assembled on Grant's side of the room. His grandmother, his parents, his sister and her husband, two aunts, an uncle, three cousins. *Former friends who are now my adversaries,* she thought.

"Hi, Daddy." Scotty waved to Grant, who got out of his seat and started walking toward them.

"Hi, partner," Tessa heard him say, but she was following Alex's lead. Without acknowledging Grant, she continued to walk with Alex. They went to the front of the room and sat down.

"Mommy?" Scotty came running up. "Can I sit with Daddy for a little while?"

Panic-stricken, Tess raised frightened eyes to Alex, who gave her a subtle nod.

"Of—of course, darling. You can sit wherever you want."

"Thanks." He darted off.

"I know you feel as if your heart's been cut out, Tess. Just remember you made it through drug withdrawal, so you can make it through this. It'll all be over before you know it."

Alex's encouraging words penetrated the layers of pain suffocating her. "If you say so," she murmured.

"I do say so," came the firm reply.

A police officer and a court reporter entered the room. There was an announcement for all to rise as Judge Larkin made his entrance. Tess knew Scotty would be watching for his cane.

Sure enough the imposing man in black robes walked in with the aid of a sturdy brown cane. His hawklike features seemed to form a permanent scowl, but her son would see beyond that, thanks to the incredible man at Tess's side.

When everyone was seated, Alex and Clive Medor were asked to approach the bench. Tessa studied the notorious attorney who, despite his plumpness and small stature, exuded a cocky self-assurance in the way he moved, held his head and gesticulated.

The little Hitler, Alex had said. Without the unattractive mustache, he would probably look quite different. But his physical characteristics were not the issue here. It was how he acted.

And how his actions affected her darling Scotty.

More than anything she wanted to turn around and look at her son, see what he was doing. Alex had told her to ignore Grant's family. He was right. Filling the courtroom with hostile relatives was just another tactic designed to intimidate her. She wouldn't let it get to her. She wouldn't!

With a nod from the judge, Alex returned to his seat. She watched him pull a brief from his case and lay it on the table in front of them.

Numbly she sat there as Grant's attorney opened the proceedings with a litany of details about his client's unhappiness in the marriage, his petition for divorce, the division of property, assets, child support, alimony.

Alex had warned her, so she knew what to expect. Nevertheless she cringed to hear herself described as a cold insensitive woman whose self-absorption emasculated the plaintiff, trampling on his tenderest feelings.

"After the birth of their son, Scotty, the defendant's depressive illness further estranged them to the point they have not had sexual relations for the past eight months of the marriage."

Tess writhed. *Nothing was private in a public court of law.*

"Medical examination has revealed that the defendant has always suffered from a form of bipolar disorder, which became more severe following the birth of their son. Defendant has been on constant medication for the past four years.

"Undaunted, the plaintiff has continued to provide for, nurture, protect and take care of his son and the defendant. When defendant wished to take their son to Hawaii for a week's vacation, the plaintiff agreed, hoping the separation would restore goodwill in the marriage."

Medor paused dramatically. "The defendant returned home a month ago and promptly filed a complaint for divorce, never once having discussed her intentions or reasons with plaintiff. The plaintiff has proof that defendant enjoyed a liaison with a man in Hawaii, Mr. Paul Wong, owner of the hotel where she and her son stayed.

"As will be proved in testimony rendered at a later date, the defendant's long-term psychiatrist is of the opinion that defendant is now taking cocaine and/or amphetamines on top of the heavy medication he has prescribed, exaggerating her manic phase."

Dr. Milhouse had planted the idea in Grant's mind. Tessa put nothing past him.

"The plaintiff has strong reason to suspect that Mr. Wong supplied defendant with drugs. Since her return, he has already attempted to make contact with defendant.

"My client is suffering extreme anxiety over the welfare of his son because his wife has stopped seeing her psychiatrist and has formed an attachment to

Mr. Wong, possibly breaking her marital vows and pursuing an adulterous relationship.''

Alex had warned her there'd be an adultery charge.

''Said psychiatrist insists that without proper monitoring and medication, her judgment is severely impaired. He is no longer her doctor of record and fears for the defendant's life, as well as her ability to mother her son. He further states that if the defendant is allowed to keep the son in her custody, there is a risk of irreparable injury to said son.

''My client has a secure home with his parents. He has prepared a bedroom for his son with all the needful things required. His parents, who are retired, will take care of his son while he works at his business. Said grandparents and extended family have a solid bond with plaintiff's son and are here in the courtroom ready to take him home, to give their financial, physical and spiritual support.''

''No. . .'' Tess whispered.

''Don't you dare faint on me,'' Alex ground out in a hushed tone. ''I haven't had *my* turn yet.''

Clawing the armrests with her fingers, she sat rigidly in her chair while Clive Medor finished crucifying her.

''Therefore, the plaintiff begs the court to grant him *immediate temporary custody, care and control* of their son, Scotty, age five, during the interim preceding trial and throughout until the court's final decision is handed down and divorce is granted. I will now offer in evidence all proof to the court starting with Exhibit A through . . ."

Dear God. Because of Dr. Milhouse's testimony, it was a foregone conclusion Scotty would be leaving court with Grant!

Now she understood why the Marsden family had come to the courtroom en masse. His family loved any excuse to have a party. She knew a huge celebration had been planned for Grant's victory and could envision Pastor Carr in attendance.

Scotty! her heart cried. Her dear little boy who'd run so eagerly to Grant a few minutes ago knew nothing about the fates ruling his destiny.

She looked up at the judge. Whatever he was thinking about her wasn't revealed on that inscrutable face. But Alex had said Judge Larkin showed wisdom in his decisions.

With nothing left but her faith in God and in Alex, all she could do was pray the judge had the wisdom of Solomon and would see into her heart. She started to shake and couldn't stop.

"Counsel for the defendant will now approach the bench."

There was no comparison between the little Hitler and her attorney. When he got up from the table, it struck Tess all over again what a wonderful human being Alex Sommerfield was. His commanding aura, his presence, the dignity he brought to the court couldn't help but be felt by every person in the room.

"Your Honor," he addressed the bench in his low vibrant voice. "My client, Tessa Marsden, the defendant in this case, comes before the court petitioning a divorce from the plaintiff on grounds of incompatibility.

"The defendant has waived her right to alimony and has given up all rights to the home her husband worked so hard to buy and maintain. All she asks is fair and equitable child support, as she wishes to obtain custody of Scott Marsden, their only issue from the marriage.

"She has just moved into an apartment with her son and is providing all the spiritual, financial and physical necessities of life."

Tess felt herself relax, ever so slightly, as he went on, "My client is a certified teacher of music. At present she is working afternoons at a local high school as a teacher's aide for the music department. Her job coincides with her son's afternoon kindergarten class so that she can send him off to school and be there for him upon his return.

"In the fall she has every expectation of being hired by the local school district for full-time teaching, which will coincide with the hours her son will attend first grade.

"My client declares that after the birth of her son, she suffered temporary postpartum depression, which was misdiagnosed as bipolar disorder, all of which will be shown in testimony during the trial."

Yes, thought Tess. *Yes, it will be shown. There'll be no question—*

"My client went to Hawaii with her son at the invitation of her brother, Mr. Winn Jenner, and his wife, Rae. The four of them made the acquaintance of Mr. Paul Wong, a man in his mid-sixties who befriended her son and subsequently found out about my client's supposed bipolar disorder.

"Not a believer in Western medicine, he challenged my client to go off all medication prescribed by her psychiatrist to find out if, in fact, she needed anything at all.

"The defendant, who suffered untold grief at being told she had a bipolar disorder, returned from Hawaii to willingly undergo drug withdrawal, knowing that her supposed severe medical condition had contributed to the breakdown of her already shaky marriage.

"She submitted herself to the care of her physician father, Dr. Richard Jenner. She chose to keep her experiment a secret until she knew one way or another if it appeared she had to stay on medication for the rest of her life."

A disturbance on the other side of the courtroom drew Tess's attention. She heard several angry voices, including Grant's, then Clive Medor was on his feet.

"Objection, Your Honor! Counsel is basing testimony on the word of defendant and defendant's father without one shred of evidence to support her fallacious and ludicrous claims."

Judge Larkin turned to Alex. "Counselor?"

"Your Honor, I've simply followed the lead of my esteemed colleague and am waiting to supply all evidence of proof at the end of my opening statement. If Counsel wishes to interrupt the court's time at this point while the evidence is examined to Counsel's satisfaction, I am in full agreement."

Tess's pain made it difficult to think with any coherence. *Dr. Milhouse had betrayed her to Grant's attorney.* He'd been betraying her to Grant for four years. She couldn't take it in.

"Counsel for the plaintiff?"

"I can't imagine what proof opposing counsel would bring before this court to support such fairy tales. In order not to waste the court's time, I would like very much to see the evidence now."

"You're close to being in contempt, Counselor."

"That was not my intention, Your Honor. I apologize."

Tess had never heard anyone less apologetic in her life. With the kind of damaging evidence her psychiatrist fed to Grant and his attorney, was it any wonder Clive Medor thought he was going to set a precedent?

Dr. Milhouse wasn't just any doctor. He held a prominent position in the psychiatric community of Colorado. Tess groaned. Fantastic as Alex was, he should never have taken her case. He was up against impossible odds.

"Both counselors will approach the bench."

Medor's cocky swagger, as he moved toward the bench, repulsed her. Then she saw Alex's mouth curve in a tiny smile that only she would have noticed before he gathered a pile of documents and carried them to the judge.

It came to her then. Alex was loving this. This is what he did for a living, what he thrived on. She couldn't imagine another person on the planet who could do what he was doing for her. If he couldn't help her, no one could. There was imply no one else like him. She loved him.

She loved him.

But there was someone in the courtroom who hated him with equal passion. Clive Medor. She could feel his animosity, hear it in his arguments with every piece of proof Alex presented to the judge. The examination seemed to take forever, and Tess feared not even Alex would be able to accomplish the impossible.

Her stomach started to churn. *I can't lose Scotty!*

"Counsel for the defendant, you may continue."

The judge had brought the conference to a close. She noted in dismay that Clive Medor's arrogant demeanor intensified as he took his seat and whispered something to Grant. Tess's eyes switched back to Alex.

"Thank you, Your Honor. As I was saying, Dr. Jenner admitted my client to the hospital in Vail, Colorado, where she was kept and monitored for forty-eight hours, then released when all danger to her heart had passed.

"Dr. Jenner and his wife nursed my client through the first difficult week of withdrawal at their mountain cabin. Within two weeks, my client was functioning normally. Since then, she has shown no signs of having a bipolar disorder.

"Indeed, she hasn't taken so much as an aspirin since her return from Hawaii a month ago. On my advice as counsel for the defendant, Dr. Jenner phoned her psychiatrist as a courtesy to him, thanking him for his help and relaying the good news that my client had recovered from any depression following the birth of her baby. He explained that my client would no longer need his services."

Alex's voice seemed more resonant than ever. "Throughout the five years of her son's life, my client has been a loving mother who has stayed home to raise her child. Despite her medical history, she has maintained a well-ordered home, completed her college education, held a job at her church and now holds a job at a local school.

"Her son is still of a young and tender age and would suffer psychological risk if removed from the home of his mother, wherever that might be. Full and liberal visitation rights for the plaintiff are already in effect. Defendant declares that the plaintiff is a wonderful father to their son. She will make every effort to see that plaintiff is with their son on an ongoing basis.

"Therefore the defendant asks the court to grant her a divorce and permanent custody of their son."

Pandemonium broke out on the other side of the room. The judge pounded his gavel. "Quiet. If I hear another outburst like that, I'll instruct the bailiff to clear the room."

He faced Alex directly. "Counsel for the defendant, the court wishes to see Scott Marsden in chambers. This session will reconvene in ten minutes." He pounded his gavel, then got up from his chair and disappeared into an adjoining room.

Alex turned to Tess, his expression sober. *Does it mean he's less than hopeful about the outcome?* Her heart plummeted. "Do you need to use the rest room, Tess?"

"N-no," she whispered through wooden lips.

"Good. Stay put and don't talk to anyone. I'll get Scotty."

Paralyzed with fear, she watched Alex walk over to Grant and invite Scotty to come with him. To her relief, Scotty seemed perfectly willing to climb off his father's lap and take hold of Alex's outstretched hand.

Together the two of them proceeded toward the door of the judge's private chambers. Just before Scotty disappeared, he turned and waved to her with his free hand.

The gesture touched her heart. She lowered her head and said a prayer.

A few minutes later a strong hand fell unexpectedly on her shoulder, sending warmth through her frozen body.

"You're going to love it," Alex murmured. "As soon as I introduced them, Scotty told the judge he thought he was brave for being in the 'Veetyam' War and asked if his leg still hurt him."

Tess gasped. "He didn't!"

"I swear it."

"Oh, Alex, I'm so frightened. Now we know why Grant came up to the cabin that night. It means Dr. Milhouse has been telli—"

"Hush." His voice was kind but firm. "Scotty's innocent display of concern for the judge probably did more for your case than all the legal jargonese in existence. No matter the picture portrayed by Medor, the judge saw in an instant what a sweet, well-adjusted child Scotty is—and that's from being in your care all his life."

Alex smiled. "Why would he jeopardize your son's emotional state by changing a situation that is obviously working well?"

"You think?" she cried, grasping for the slightest ray of hope.

He gave her a pensive nod. "Hold on, Tess. The end is in sight. I'll go get you some water."

CHAPTER TWELVE

EVERYONE BUT TESS had cleared the courtroom. Even if Alex hadn't warned her about staying put, she couldn't have moved. Scotty was in the room behind the judge's rostrum. When her son came out, she wanted to be there for him.

"You're not going to get away with this, Tessa."

The voice of anger.

Grant had slipped back into the courtroom and come down the aisle. She refused to look at him. "Haven't we put each other through enough pain? It's in the judge's hands now."

"You don't know what pain is." His voice shook. "But you're going to find out when Scotty goes home with me this afternoon. I can hardly wait to watch the judge's decision wipe that smug look off your face." His venom stupefied her. "You can't imagine the pleasure I'm going to derive listening to you beg for time with my son. It'll be a first for a Jenner."

"It'll be a *last* for a Marsden when I ask the court to have you banned from the rest of these proceedings for harassing my client."

The wintry voice was Alex's. Thank God. She couldn't have taken any more right then.

"Court's not in session, and this is none of your business, Mr. God Almighty."

Tess bowed her head. She'd never seen or heard Grant like this. Not even at the cabin.

"One more word and I'll obtain an order charging you with harassment." Voiced with deadly intent, Alex's warning was no idle threat and Grant knew it. Even Tess shivered before her estranged husband bristled in defeat, then stormed off.

By now the bailiff had reappeared and people were starting to file back in.

Alex sat down next to her and put a paper cup filled with water in her hands. "Drink every drop."

She didn't need urging. Fear had parched her throat. "Thank you," she murmured when she'd drained it. "I don't mean just for the water."

His eyes darkened to cobalt. "I know exactly what you meant."

He *did* know. He knew everything.

"All rise. Court is now in session, the Honorable Rutherford T. Larkin presiding."

With thudding heart, Tess fastened her attention on the judge. As he emerged from chambers, she expected Scotty to come out with him, but there was no sign of her son.

"Alex? Where is he?"

"Probably trying to decide which flavor lollipop he wants."

She sucked in her breath. What would she have done without Alex? *What in heaven's name would she have done without him?*

The judge sat down and put on his glasses. He leaned forward and eyed everyone in the room.

"In the divorce action that has come before this court, the issue in the countersuit is whether the pretrial evidence supports that the *best* interests of the child are served by awarding both temporary and permanent custody of him to the plaintiff, his father."

The blood pounded in her ears. She was terrified the judge was going to give Scotty to Grant. That was probably why her little boy hadn't made an appearance.

"After weighing the points in the record and taking into account the child's testimony," the judge continued, "the court has determined that the pretrial evidence is less than substantial or conclusive for either party and therefore orders plaintiff, defendant and son to undergo a custody evaluation to be performed by Counseling Services, and to seek expert advice of the social worker assigned to the case.

"To further illuminate the court's understanding, both plaintiff and defendant shall undergo psychological testing. The defendant shall also submit to a psychiatric examination by a court-appointed psychiatrist. This case will reconvene for trial April the eighth, when all findings are recorded and presented as expert testimony."

He paused for a breath. Tess was holding hers. "Concerning the matter of *temporary* custody, the court notes that said child has always been at home with the mother and has derived some substantial benefit.

"Removing the child from his present home could cause psychological risk greater than the existing risk as reported by the inconclusive evidence in this hearing. Therefore, until the date of trial, it is the decision of the court that the son, Scott, remain in the temporary care and custody of the mother."

Tess jerked in her seat. Prepared to hear just the opposite, she was afraid she'd pass out, anyway, from too much happiness. Alex must have thought so, too, because he reached for her hand and clasped it hard before letting it go. "I told you the judge was a wise man. Take a couple of deep breaths."

There was an anguished cry from someone in Grant's family. It sounded very much like Nana Marsden. Tess was thankful Scotty wasn't in the room to hear her. The judge pounded his gavel. "Bailiff, escort her outside. Counselor, do what you must to keep order or I'll find you in contempt."

"Yes, Your Honor." The little Hitler still didn't sound at all remorseful.

Out of the corner of her eye, Tess saw Grampa Marsden help his distraught wife to her feet. They left the room, followed by the officer. Knowing Grant's mother, she had probably spent weeks getting everything ready for Scotty. Grant was her pride and joy, and she adored her grandson.

Tess's estrangement from Grant's parents was another ramification of the divorce that tore her apart. She loved his family. So did Scotty.

The judge cleared his throat. "It is further ordered that full and liberal visitation rights continue to be strictly maintained and enforced. Both plaintiff and defendant will refrain from making derogatory or inflammatory remarks about the other in front of their son. Both parties will actively support the other in building an environment that encourages child/ parental harmony. Counselor for the defendant will now escort said son from chambers. Court is adjourned."

The sound of the gavel brought an end to the proceedings. With the swiftness of a panther, Alex followed the judge's retreat. The second he emerged from the other room with her son in hand, Tess flew out of her seat.

"Scotty!"

He let go of Alex and hurried toward her, his mouth full of candy. "Are you all right?"

He nodded his head. "The judge is nice. I got to see his scar."

Tess's heart swelled so she couldn't talk. Alex, sensing her needs as always, turned to Scotty.

"Your father and grandparents are out in the hall waiting to see you. What would you like to do? Go home with them and let your father bring you back to your mom's tonight?"

Although Tess didn't want to be separated from Scotty right now, she saw the wisdom in Alex's suggestion. His humanity made her love him all the more.

Scotty started to nod, then stopped. "Can we go to that deli you told me about first?"

"I was hoping you'd say that. I'm hungry."

"Me, too. Are you hungry, Mommy?"

"Starved."

"Then it's settled," Alex murmured, capturing Tess's gaze. She knew that everything she felt for this marvelous man was there in her eyes. But for once, she didn't try to hide it or look away. She couldn't.

He'd accomplished the impossible. He'd won her two more months for certain with her son, something no other attorney could have done. But he'd taken her case on faith. He'd believed in her. No amount of money could pay the debt she owed him.

In a trembling voice she asked, "How do I thank you?"

"You can start by joining your son and me for cheesecake."

Her heart began to run away with her. It was an outing of sorts. She planned to make the most of it.

"Scotty?" She leaned over and cupped his face in her hands. "Run and find Daddy and tell him that Uncle Winn will take you to Nana Marsden's as soon as you've had lunch. Tell him you can sleep over if you want to. I'll come and get you tomorrow."

"Can't I sleep with you?"

"Of course, honey. Daddy can bring you back later tonight. I'll wait here while you tell him."

"Okay."

"I'll take Scotty to find him," Alex offered. "When the two of you are ready, meet me on the top steps outside the courthouse and we'll walk over to the deli."

WHILE ALEX WAITED, he took out his cellular phone and called his office.

"Burt. The first round went as I expected. Now we're going to celebrate. Call Sol's Deli and ask for Hannah. Tell her there's something special in it for her if she finds me a table in the back for three." He dictated their order. "I should be in the office by two."

After discussing some other matters of business, he clicked off and pulled out the small address book he always carried. It was time to call the Jenners and put them out of their misery, let them enjoy the calm before the next storm.

They were absolutely thrilled at his news and couldn't thank Alex enough. He told them that the three of them were on their way to Sol's Deli and wondered if Winn could pick Tess and Scotty up there in about forty-five minutes.

"He'll be there," a tearful Mrs. Jenner asserted.

"Alex—" Dr. Jenner's voice broke "—you can't know what this means to us."

For once in his career, Alex thought that he did. Tessa Marsden had already become the most important person in his life. The admission was at once terrifying and exhilarating.

"Tess will give you the particulars when you see her. We'll talk again soon."

Alex stared into the distance without seeing anything. Every Jenner was a Thoroughbred. Sometimes Thoroughbreds suffered the worst kind of pain. Maybe it was because the gods were jealous of their many gifts and so sent them the harshest tests.

Tess had come close to the fire today, but she hadn't yet walked through the wall of flames. But when the time came, she wouldn't have to do it alone. No matter the risk, Alex had made up his mind that they'd face the fiery furnace together. No matter the outcome, she was his soul mate. He was hers. He knew it in the very essence of his being. To think there'd been a time when he'd mocked such an absurd notion.

One day they would stand before each other, a man and a woman, free to claim what the gods in their cruelty had so far forbidden them. One day—

"Nice work, Counselor."

Alex didn't have to turn around to know the little Hitler was behind him wearing his Cheshire-cat grin. "Medor."

"I have to admit what you pulled off in there was classic, but you and I both know you've exhausted everything in your bag of tricks. When we meet again, what will you do for an encore?"

You'll find out long before we face each other in the courtroom. "Since you answered your own question, I'm surprised you asked. Have a good day."

Medor stayed planted. "You were a little rough on my client during recess."

"He was a little rough on mine. Just doing my job."

"You're a bastard, Counselor."

"I've been called worse."

"We both know she's a frigid highbrow bitch who emasculated him on his wedding night and then only allowed him the use of her body once or twice a year as duty warranted."

Medor was so worked up he'd forgotten to be careful. His carelessness clarified Alex's suspicion that Tess's wedding night had been something hideous. Something she'd alluded to, but hadn't talked about. Maybe one day, she'd be able to really unburden herself to him.

In any event, Medor had just given away Grant Marsden's motive for filing for divorce six years back. Apparently his sexual frustration had led him to the brink of divorcing Tess, but at the last minute, he couldn't go through with it.

Alex had the strong suspicion that Grant Marsden saw his wife as a trophy and would rather stay in a bad marriage than admit to the world he couldn't hang on to his prize. It certainly explained why Tess never learned that he'd filed for divorce. If she had, she might have left him and never looked back. Grant couldn't have stood the humiliation.

Alex smiled with satisfaction. Medor's carelessness was going to cost him during the trial.

"Alex!" Scotty called to him from the doors. Tessa wouldn't be far behind.

Medor's eyes held a malicious gleam. "So it's *Alex* already. Well, well, well. Aren't *we* cozy."

"It's getting old, Medor. See you in court." Alex picked up his briefcase and crossed to Scotty.

"Where's your mother?" If Grant Marsden had cornered her...

"She's coming."

Alarmed that nerves had made her ill, he said, "Let's go inside and wait for her." As he reached for Scotty's hand, he saw her beautiful face through the glass door. Her effect on him was like a shot of adrenaline directly to the heart.

She hurried outside. "I didn't come out before because I saw Grant's attorney talking to you. I decided to wait until he'd gone."

"We were clearing up last-minute business," he said, thankful her instincts were on full alert. "Shall we go?"

Making sure Scotty stayed in the middle, he indicated their destination and they headed for the corner. Alex was grateful for the milder weather they were having. Since the freeze had ended, they could walk without fear of slipping.

While Scotty happily chattered away, Alex found himself distracted by Tess's shining hair, glowing face and the elegant way she carried herself. Every so often she turned her head and smiled at him. Her eyes radiated a light that needed no translation. She still had her son at her side. Alex knew she was trying to thank him every way she knew how.

A part of him sensed those smiles were attempting to convey another message. One more subtle, but there all the same.

When they reached the deli, Hannah came up the minute she saw him. "Follow me, Counselor."

"Bless you, Hannah," he said sotto voce as she led them through the crowd to the very spot he'd had in mind.

She winked at him before approaching Scotty. "Today's menu features hot dogs, hot cider and cheesecake. How does that sound?"

"Yum." Scotty's face lit up.

"For you big kids—" her sparkling eyes took in both him and Tess "—you'll have to do with spinach quiche."

"I hate spinach," Scotty said. "Do you like it, Mommy?"

"In quiche I do. Thank you."

With the ordering done, Alex lounged back in the chair feeling pleasantly tired and at peace with the world. Why not? The pretrial had gone as planned.

Everyone he cared about was sitting at the table with him.

Scotty delivered a running commentary about things Alex had never noticed before, like Hannah's uniform and the design of the floor tiles. Alex got a big kick out of Scotty. He was a great kid and exactly the kind of son any man would cherish.

Grant Marsden was luckier than he knew, but what Medor unintentionally let slip today convinced Alex that the countersuit for custody had been motivated by something much less noble than a desire to father his son twenty-four hours a day.

"I called your parents."

"I know," she said as Hannah brought them their food. "I called them, too. Thank you for being so considerate."

"Since I requested that they stay away from the courtroom, it was the least I could do."

She helped Scotty get catsup out of the bottle, then her golden brown eyes leveled on him. "I'm so glad they weren't there."

Alex had devoured his quiche and had started on his dessert. "The trial is the place where you'll want their support."

"Mommy? Are we divorced now?" Scotty finished the last of his cheesecake and licked his fork.

"We will be in a couple of months."

"Scotty—" Alex reached in his pocket "—here's a quarter. I can see a gum-ball machine over by the cash register."

The diversionary tactic worked. Scotty took the coin from Alex and ran off calling, "Thanks!" over his shoulder.

Tess paled. "Why did you send Scotty away? Is something wrong? Does it have to do with whatever Clive Medor was saying to you outside the courthouse?"

Alex grimaced and pushed his half-eaten cheesecake away. "Forget Medor. Tess, it's *possible* you'll be divorced in two months at the end of the custody trial, but I don't want you counting on it."

"Why?" She sounded aghast.

"Judges are strange animals. Their timetable differs from ours. They adjudicate at their own discretion."

A shadow withered her expression. "So what you're saying is, it could be much longer."

His hand made a fist on his thigh beneath the table. "I'm saying, don't speculate on a date."

"How long *could* he take?"

Alex had been waiting for that question. The answer had been eating at him for weeks. "Longer than you want."

"That's not an answer."

"It's the only one I've got, but Scotty doesn't need to know that."

She wouldn't look at him. Before he knew it, she'd gotten up from the table. "Thank you for all you've done." Her voice broke. "If it wasn't for you, Scotty wouldn't be with me now. I don't even want to think what my life would be like without you—without your help. The food was delicious, but we have to go. I imagine Winn is out front waiting.''

Alex rose to his feet, tossing his napkin on the table. ''I'll walk you and Scotty to the car.''

''No!'' she cried in panic. ''Don't!''

In the next instant, her profile was turned away from him and she fled the restaurant on those gorgeous legs of hers. He hoped Tess's reaction meant that a long separation was as unpalatable to her as it was to him.

Whatever their private hells, this was only the beginning.

CHAPTER THIRTEEN

"IS THERE A CHANCE Tessa's going to win?"

Clive paused before getting into his Porsche in the underground parking lot of the courthouse.

"Your wife doesn't have a hope in hell, Grant."

"That's what you said about the pretrial."

"I know you and your family are disappointed about the outcome. But today's round was only a minor setback. No one's fault. Even Dr. Milhouse didn't know what she was up to—this business of her withdrawing from the medication he had her on. It was a cheap trick orchestrated by her attorney at the last minute."

"You think the psychiatrist appointed by the court is going to see through their ruse?"

"Let's get something straight here, Grant. Milhouse is vice president of the Colorado Psychiatric Association right now, due to be president in a couple of months. He's an institution in his own right and has been your wife's doctor for four years. Don't forget that her own well-known father referred her to him in the first place. Milhouse is going to be our key witness."

"I know."

"Grant, I wouldn't have taken your case if I didn't know I could win. Your job is to sail through your psychological evaluation and come out smelling and looking squeaky clean."

"I'm not worried about that."

"Then what's in your craw, boy? The expert witnesses are going to make mincemeat of her." *Particularly Lew Orton, the social worker at Counseling Services.* He'd tear her apart, piece by piece, till there was nothing left.

"But what if she really *is* off all medication?"

"Then the judge will string the case out to see just how long it takes her illness to come back. She's not going anywhere. In the meantime, she has to survive the group-therapy sessions I'm setting up. Have you ever sat in on one of those?"

"No."

"Count your blessings. It's like walking through a mine field. She'll break before she's halfway through it."

His client ground his teeth. "Just *once* I'd like to see that happen to Tessa."

"I hear you. Have patience. You think she's psycho now, you're not going to recognize her by the trial. Someone will have to peel her up off the floor."

Clive was looking forward to that day. *Not even Sommerfield would want her then.*

"WELL, TESSA. Thank you for joining us today."

The six other men and women in the therapy session stared at her as she walked in the door and sat down. She knew she wasn't late. It was ten o'clock exactly. But every word that came out of Mr. Orton's mouth was either sarcasm or innuendo.

At her first session three weeks ago, the social worker had pretended to be her friend. When she broke down because she was so frightened of losing Scotty, he told her he understood exactly how she felt. She'd been completely taken in by his sympathetic attitude.

But in the three subsequent sessions, Orton had turned into a different person, pecking away parts of her like a vulture in an eating frenzy. She almost hadn't shown up today, fearing she couldn't take any more.

If it hadn't been for Winn and Rae, who'd come by the apartment and helped build up her confidence to face today's final session, she couldn't have made it as far as the front doors.

Counseling Services occupied a bungalow across the street from the hospital where Tess had gone for her appointments with Dr. Milhouse. The place was a hellhole. No carpet, no curtains, rickety furniture, dark wood, depressing atmosphere. Scotty had said how ugly it was when he'd been forced to come for tests.

What went on inside the walls was so ghastly Tess couldn't believe the court approved. So many times she'd wanted to call Alex and tell him of Mr. Orton's cruel relentless treatment of her, but she didn't dare. She had to prove she was mentally fit to handle the abuse he heaped on her. Something told her the trial was going to be like this.

There were days after these and the psychiatric sessions—as well as the unorthodox late-evening home visits by the bearded social worker—when she wondered if she'd be dead before morning.

She wanted Alex, craved his calming optimism, his goodness. Three weeks without seeing or talking to him had convinced her that what she felt for him wasn't going to go away.

She really *was* in love with him.

The day at the deli had illuminated that salient fact for her. She'd come so close to revealing her true feelings she'd run from the deli in absolute panic, promising herself to leave him alone until they went to trial.

Alex's inability—or was it a refusal?—to answer her question about when the divorce would come through made her ask another teacher at school whose husband was an attorney. To her horror, she'd learned that obtaining a divorce could take as long as two years, maybe more, depending on the case.

Two years? She couldn't comprehend it. And after the trial, which was only two weeks away, she'd have no excuse to see Alex or talk to him at all.

What if her instincts were wrong? What if she'd misread as desire what she sometimes glimpsed in Alex's eyes when she entered a room? Had the concern he'd shown her been the same concern he showed every client? Did he comfort his other female clients in the same way? Did he touch them? Worry over them? Make them feel cherished?

"Tess? Where are you?"

"Right here," she murmured.

"I asked you a question."

"I'm sorry. I didn't hear you."

"You do a lot of that," said one of the men.

"What do you mean?"

"I agree," another man chimed in. "She's always aloof. Like you can barely tolerate any of us."

"It's typical of rich people," a woman over in the corner interjected.

"Rich?" Tess repeated in disbelief.

"We all know your dad's a doctor."

"They bring in the bucks, that's for sure."

No one had ever explained to Tess what these people were doing here. She had no idea if they were Mr. Orton's regular patients, or if they were people like herself undergoing evaluation by court order. But it was becoming clear that they all thought her worthless and incapable of being a decent mother.

How much more, God?

Mr. Orton sat back in the dented folding chair. "We want to hear about how visitation went over the weekend."

"Did your little boy cry over the phone again because he wanted to come home?" This from a woman with curly black hair who seemed to take great delight in hurting her.

"We're waiting for your answer, Tessa."

If she refused to cooperate, Mr. Orton would report it to the court. If she lied, Grant would refute it. If she told the truth, they'd pounce on her. Struggling for breath she said, "Yes. He called me."

"Why? What do you say to him that makes him go to the phone every time he drives off with his daddy? Scotty's *his* flesh and blood, too, and has every right to be with him."

"Of course he does," Tess agreed.

"What did your little boy want this time?"

"Just to talk."

"Hell. He's home with you ninety-nine percent of the time. You're a selfish bitch. If you were my wife, I'd teach you a thing or two."

"Watch your language, Dave," Mr. Orton admonished, but Tess could tell he was enjoying this. She was so frightened and repulsed she didn't think she could sit here any longer.

The others laughed. "That's why you're in here, Dave."

"Have you been bothering her again since you got out of jail?"

"We're not through with Tessa," their mentor broke in. "What time did your husband bring Scotty home?"

She bowed her head. "He didn't. He kept him overnight again."

"Oh." Everyone pretended to feel bad.

"He broke visitation rules, Lew," another man chimed in. "Oh, dear. What a catastrophe. What's Mommy going to do all alone?"

Lew Orton stared pointedly at Tess. "How did you react to that?"

"When it got to be eleven o'clock, I called him to find out if something was wrong."

"Because he was late with his own kid?" another one of the group fired at her.

"Did you think something terrible was going to happen to your kid because his father got to see him for another day longer?"

She bit her lip to keep herself from screaming at the top of her lungs. "No. Grant's a good father. But Scotty has had a hard time getting used to visitation, and he expected to be home Sunday night. I was worried until I talked to him."

"If you were my wife—"

"Shut up, Dave. We're not talking about you. We're talking about Miss Hoity-Toity sitting over there. You're the kind of woman that turns their sons into belly-aching mama's boys. If he grows up with you, he'll turn out to be gay."

"*How dare you!*"

"Oh! Forgive me, your highness." One of the men stood up and bowed to her. Everyone laughed.

"Excuse me."

"Where are you going, Tessa?"

"To the rest room."

"Sally? Go with her," Mr. Orton spoke to the woman who'd been merciless to her. "Leave your purse on your chair."

Tess dropped it and ran for the rest room. But she only made it as far as the sink before she retched. Since she hadn't been able to eat all day, nothing came up but bile. She stood there shaking until her stomach quieted, then rinsed her mouth and face.

The other woman lounged against the wall and watched her. "I hope you're as rich as Lew says you are. You're going to need the best attorney there is."

"I *have* the best attorney there is."

"You're not supposed to know, but we've been giving you a hard time on purpose. If you tell Lew I told you, I'll deny it. Better get back in there before he suspects something."

After five grueling weeks, one person had had the courage to tell her what was really going on. Tess grabbed hold of the other woman's arm. White-faced, she whispered, "Thank you for that."

"Personally I think your husband should get the kid. They're too much trouble, and you've got everything else going for you. But what's been going on in there today isn't right. Hey—I work at Top Stop on Applewood. Call me sometime."

Tess silently thanked her maker and followed the other woman out. But as soon as she stepped into the hall, she came face-to-face with Mr. Orton.

"Here's your purse. Although today's session is over, I want to see you in my office."

Her dread of having to spend another second in his company gave her the shakes, but she didn't have a choice.

Once they were seated he said, "You've been resisting us in these sessions. Your outburst was just another case in point. When you can't handle something you don't like, you try intimidation, which you do very successfully I might add. It's a controlling technique that would paralyze a child.

"When that doesn't work, you run away because you're out of control and don't want anyone to see it. I'm recommending to the court that you spend more time with me before I write up my findings. I'm also going to have you put on medication for—"

"*No!*" Tess leapt to her feet and started for the door. "The court stipulated five weeks of therapy and I've complied. As for medication, I will never take it again in my life. You can put that in your report to the court, *Lew!*"

"BOSS?" SAID BURT. "Mrs. Jenner is here without an appointment. Shall I—"

Alex cut him off. "The Jenners can interrupt me any time. Send her in."

"You have a conference call in five minutes."

"We'll see," was all he said before he got up from his desk and strode across the room to greet her. Three empty weeks without a word from Tess had pretty well destroyed his peace of mind. Now her mother was here, unannounced. He felt like a fist had just landed in his gut.

"Come in, Wilma."

Over the past month there'd been a toll on the woman from whom Tess had derived so much of her beauty. Grief was written all over her face.

"Thank you, Alex. I hope I haven't put you out too much."

"Not at all. How's Tess?"

"Not good. That's why I'm here. She's at school and doesn't know I've come. If she'd known my intentions, she'd never have let me."

Alex didn't like the sound of that for a variety of reasons he couldn't afford to analyze now. "Sit down and tell me what's wrong."

"Tess went to her last therapy session today. What's gone on there is criminal, but she hasn't wanted to say a word to you because she's tried to be brave. She's also terrified that if this gets out, there'll be retaliation in the courtroom. But after what she told me about this morning's session, my husband and I are ready to bring a lawsuit against Counseling Services and Lew Orton for unconscionable behavior.''

Alex let out the breath he was holding. He'd tried to warn Tess. "I want to hear everything, but first let me tell my paralegal to reschedule a call."

Once he'd given Burt instructions, he reached for his pen and pad. "Go ahead, Wilma."

Both mother and daughter enjoyed a rare rapport. If he closed his eyes, he could hear Tess in her mother's voice. She began relating the details of Tess's sessions, often using some of her daughter's expressions.

He thought he knew what was coming. But with every word Wilma spoke, his anger grew until it reached white-hot intensity.

"That's not all, Alex. Before Tess left Orton's office today, he told her she'd have to undergo more sessions. He also told her she'd have to be put on medication to control her."

Alex restrained the urge to get up and put his fist through the wall by clinging to the chair's armrests. "You're right, Wilma. He's shown flagrant abuse of his office, and there are legal ways to deal with him, which we'll talk about at a later date."

Lew Orton sounded like a woman hater. He sounded like Clive Medor. The two men obviously had a scheme going. Custody evaluations by private establishments were used all the time in courts of law. Obviously not all of them operated on the up-and-up.

"Don't worry about your daughter, Wilma. When you go home, you can tell her she's fulfilled the stipulations of the court order. She never has to deal with Orton or Counseling Services again."

"Thank God. Tess can't take any more. Neither can we."

"Wilma, if anyone from that outfit should show up at your home or Tess's apartment, don't even open the door. Do you have caller ID?" She nodded. "How about Tess?"

"Yes. We insisted."

"Good. If anyone should phone you, ignore it. Any correspondence, bring it to me."

"Thank you, Alex. I feel so much better."

They both stood.

"Tess should've come to me the moment she felt them ganging up on her, but I know why she didn't. She's trying to prove to the world that she's strong and capable."

Wilma's eyes misted over. "My daughter *is* strong and capable, and far braver than I could ever be. But when I think of what she's been through, what she still has to face, I don't know how anyone could survive it."

Without conscious thought, Alex put an arm around her shoulders. "Just as you're fighting for Tess, she's fighting for Scotty. I've always heard that

a mother fighting for her young has awesome powers, and now I'm seeing it. Tess's going to come out
on top, whole and happy. You'll see."

"When I hear you talk like that, I can believe it."
Wilma hugged him back, then pulled away and wiped
her eyes. "I've got to get home before she does.
Thank you for dropping everything to see me."

"My privilege." He walked her out to reception.
"Do me a favor. Tell Tess to call me, no matter how
trivial the reason. She doesn't have to be brave for me.
I want to know how she's doing."

"She and Scotty are coming over tonight to spend
the evening with us. I'll tell her what you said. Bless
you, Alex."

"Burt," he said as soon as she'd gone, "what did
you do about that conference call?"

"It's rescheduled for tomorrow at the same time."

"Good. There's a pad of notes on my desk that
need transcribing as soon as you can get to them."

"Okay. Anything else?"

"Yes. I'm due in court in fifteen minutes. If Tessa
Marsden should phone, call me on the cellular. Anything else can wait until I call you."

"Good luck tomorrow."

"Thanks, Burt. Remind me to give you another
pair of tickets to the Nuggets' game."

AT FIVE-THIRTY, after a big win in the Penman case,
Alex shook hands with opposing counsel and left.

Normally he and his colleagues would spend some time chatting about the judge's decision.

But tonight Alex couldn't get out of the courthouse fast enough. Not only was Tess's ordeal with Orton on his mind, the newspapers would have hit the stands. In a few minutes, he'd know if his tip had produced results.

Not willing to wait until he arrived home, he bought a paper on the corner. By the time he'd reached his car, he'd found the article he was hoping to see on the front page of the local section.

PROMINENT PSYCHIATRIST TO ANSWER CHARGES.

Alex scanned the test with glee, elated that the reporter for the *Post*, Jerry Rideout, had run with the evidence Alex had shown him. When it came to ferreting out a story, Rideout had a reputation for being a pit bull.

All Alex had had to do was supply him with a starter list of phone numbers, and those jaws had gone for the jugular. His long-reaching tentacles had stretched in every direction: the Drug Enforcement Agency, the state occupational licensing bureau, the American Medical Association, the Colorado State Psychiatric Association and Mountaincrest Hospital administration, to name a few.

Rideout had run a thorough check on Milhouse's background—where he'd gone to medical school, where he'd done his internship and residency. According to the article, no one in the top echelons was available for comment. The president of the state psychiatric association hadn't returned any of Rideout's calls.

Milhouse, as well as the psychiatric community, had to be squirming. And Medor should be undergoing cardiac arrest about now.

Alex had never thought of himself as a bloodthirsty person. But what Milhouse had done to hundreds of women's lives was criminal.

What he'd done to Tess's life, the impact on her husband and Scotty, the damage to their marriage, the pain to their families, none of it bore thinking about.

Before Alex went home, he had a very special lady to thank in person. He'd stop at a florist and buy some long-stemmed roses. Yellow maybe, for the sunshine she spread to everyone who knew her?

On second thought, red, for courage. It had taken great courage to do what Sadie did, then allow Alex to run with it. He would never forget.

"YOOHOO, MOM? Dad? Tessie? Anyone?"

"We're in the study, Winn."

"Mom—" Tess eyed her mother anxiously "—don't say anything to him about what happened to me this morning."

"I wouldn't dream of it. Winn'd probably go to Counseling Services tomorrow and strangle that despicable man with his bare hands."

She wouldn't put it past Winn, either. After recovering from the initial shock of learning that her mother had gone to Alex's office, Tess was relieved he was going to protect her from Mr. Orton. And a secret part of her was thrilled that he wanted her to call him. The fantasies she'd woven about Alex were growing stronger.

Suddenly Winn burst into the study, jarring her from her thoughts. "Where's Dad?" His obvious excitement caused Tess and her mom to exchange a curious glance.

"He ran an errand with Scotty. He'll be right back."

"Have any of you read tonight's paper?"

"I'm afraid it's still out on the front porch."

"You're not going to believe it! Wait right there!" He dashed back out again.

Guilt assailed Tess. Her hideous divorce had managed to take precedence over everything. The entire fabric of their lives had been destroyed because of her.

No longer could her father come home from a hard day's work and sit down to read the paper or watch TV to relax. Now he had a daughter to console. Tonight he'd entered the study just as Tess was relating more of what happened at Counseling Services. It simply had to stop.

"Get a load of this!" Winn flew back into the room with the paper already pulled apart. A wolfish grin lit up his face. "You two are going to love this."

"What?" they both said.

"Are you ready?"

Tess smiled in spite of her pain. Winn's exuberance for life, his flare for the dramatic, made him wonderful to be around. She adored him.

"'Dr. Howard Milhouse, prominent Colorado psychiatrist and president-elect of the Colorado Psychiatric Association, has been brought up on charges of misdiagnosing more than ninety percent of his patients with bipolar disorder, better known as manic-depression.

"'Further investigation has revealed that Dr. Milhouse has indiscriminately been dispensing heavy addicting tranquilizers that far exceed the normal range of dosage.'"

"*Winn!*" Tess shrieked and jumped to her feet.

"It gets better. Listen to this. 'Records from the outpatient files at Mountaincrest Hospital going back three years reveal more of the same shocking numbers, all of whom are female patients. Hospital officials have declined to answer questions. The state psychiatric association has refused comment until the matter has been thoroughly investigated. Formal charges are pending.'"

Tess slipped under Winn's arm to read aloud the rest of the article. "'AMA official, noted psychiatrist Dr. Lawrence Early, of Delaware, says: "bipolar disorder affects approximately ten percent of the average patient load of a psychiatrist at any given time. The odds of this disorder exceeding twenty percent are beyond the range of probability and enter the range of impossibility.' "

"I don't believe it." Tess felt her brother's arms go around her. By now their mother was reading the rest of the article.

" 'Dr. Milhouse hasn't answered his telephone and can't be rea—' "

"Mommy! We're back!"

"Oh, Scotty." Tess almost choked on his name. The second he flew into the room, she reached for him.

"Richard, darling," said Wilma, "we have the most amazing news!"

"Mom's right. This is going to knock your socks off, Dad." Winn handed him the newspaper.

When her father finally raised his head, his face had gone white. Tears glistened on his cheeks.

"Tess—" the anguish in his tone wrenched her heart "—to think I referred you to him."

He gave a choked sob and began to weep in earnest. Tess let go of Scotty and wrapped her arms around him. "Daddy, it wasn't your fault. Don't. Please." She held him for long minutes.

"What's the matter with Grampa, Mommy?" asked Scotty.

Wilma caught hold of his hand. "We've had some wonderful news, and Grampa is just, well, overwhelmed. Why don't you and I go into the kitchen and make popcorn for everyone? We're going to have a celebration."

"Goody!"

When her father's weeping subsided, Tess eased away from him. "If you and Winn will excuse me for a minute, there's something I have to do."

"When you talk to Alex," her father divined with a knowing gleam in his eye, "tell him—" his voice broke "—tell him how grateful this parent is that he had the courage to take your case in the face of such impossible odds. In my book, he's what a real hero is all about, my darling girl."

In the grip of so much emotion, Tess could only nod. "Tell him ditto for me," Winn said, and his white smile was the last thing she saw before fleeing the study for the upstairs bedroom, where she could talk to Alex in private.

Her arrival coincided with the ringing of the telephone. *Alex!* She grabbed the receiver and without thinking, said his name.

"My attorney was right. You and your attorney *do* have a thing going."

Her legs buckled. It was Grant.

Hearing his bitter voice was like being pushed out of an airplane into an inky black void. She couldn't form words.

"Don't think what you saw in the paper about Dr. Milhouse changes anything about our case. You're not fit to raise Scotty. We both know whose cheap shot this was. You'll never get away with it, Tessa. Your father can't buy your way out of this one, not even if he hired F. Lee Bailey."

"Where's your humanity, Grant?" she couldn't refrain from asking. "Doesn't it mean anything to you that I was misdiagnosed, that we were all put through four years of hell for nothing?"

"If you want to talk about hell, let's talk about our honeymoon. It was downhill all the way from there. But you're going to pay when the court has you put away so you can't be with Scotty." Grant was out of control.

"I'm not going anywhere, Grant, and certainly not without my child!" She hung up on him, her mind still reeling from the amazing revelations about Dr. Milhouse.

More than ever she needed to talk to Alex, but when she called, she got his answering machine. She left a brief message. Her fierce disappointment at not finding him home fueled a brand-new emotion. Jealousy.

She'd been so caught up in her own problems it hadn't dawned on her until now that he might be taking a night off from his practice to be with a woman.

She stayed in her room for a time, thinking about Milhouse's crime, Grant's call, but mostly about how she could've let herself get so wrapped up in Alex. She had to be out of her mind....

"Tess?"

She got up from the bed and walked over to the door. "Yes, Mom?"

"You have a visitor, honey."

She stayed in her room for a time, quieting their billowed voice, Grand call, her man...

CHAPTER FOURTEEN

ALEX HAD STAYED at Sadie's later than he'd intended. When he'd called his condo for phone messages, he'd heard Tessa's voice and found himself driving straight over to the Jenners' home. The spectacular estate blended with the landscape, inside and out. An amazing amalgam of glass, wood and the elements.

He'd never had a reason to come here. He really didn't have one now. Not even the break of the news story on Milhouse warranted a nocturnal visit to his client's parents' home. But a compulsion stronger than caution kept him from returning to his condo.

The cause of that compulsion was coming down the stairs now. She was dressed casually in navy warm-ups, her long hair in a braid flung with careless grace over her shoulder.

When she saw him, she hesitated before taking another step and her eyes met his in stunned surprise. He got a suffocating feeling in his chest. If no one else had been in the house, he would have met her halfway and kissed her senseless.

"Alex, I—I didn't know you were coming." She sounded as breathless as he felt.

"I didn't, either." Lord. It was a mistake to have come here. "I was out when I checked my messages and discovered that you'd called. It was a last-second decision to drop by here on my way home. I imagined you saw the story on Milhouse in the evening paper. I presume that's why you called me."

The slight pause before she said yes thrilled him.

Damn the case. Damn the intangible barrier that prevented them from acting and behaving like two people in love. They *were* in love. Her eyes beckoned him every time she glanced his way. He felt as if he was in a straitjacket. Her suffering could be no different.

She joined him at the bottom of the staircase, her hand still welded to the railing. "The article exposing Dr. Milhouse is nothing short of a miracle." Her whole countenance glowed. The horror of her morning session with one of Medor's cronies had been wiped away. Temporarily, anyway.

"Yes. It couldn't have come at a better time."

"Will it help my case?"

Inches apart from her, he watched the fast-beating pulse in her throat with fascination. Her skin was smooth, flawless. "It's certainly not going to hurt it."

Her joy in his answer was short-lived. "Grant called a few minutes ago. He intimated that Dad had something to do with that story getting in the paper.

He warned me that it wouldn't make any difference, that I was still unfit to keep Scotty."

"I'm not surprised. It would take a mature human being to refrain from striking out at this late date."

If Medor hadn't suffered a stroke by now, Alex reckoned, he was close. His whole case rested on Milhouse's testimony. With the doctor's reputation in question, Medor would have to come up with a new battle plan. And he didn't have much time.

That was what Alex had been counting on. The revelation about Milhouse this close to trial meant he'd really have to scramble. In his haste to regroup, he was bound to grow careless, make mistakes.

Alex was ready for him.

"Tess, is this coming weekend Scotty's visitation?"

"No." She seemed startled by the change of subject.

"Then there's nothing more for you to do until your trial. If you want my advice, take Scotty and go away for a few days, just the two of you. Your parents' cabin in the mountains would be an ideal spot to enjoy this time with your son. Put everything out of your mind and relax. There's still a ton of snow up there. Have fun. Ski. Sled. Build a snowman."

Just don't tell me if you do, because I won't have the willpower to stay away.

"Tess, darling?" called Wilma. "Are you going to keep Alex standing in the foyer all night? We're dying to talk to him."

Alex watched her blush scarlet, a phenomenon he'd only read about in books but had never witnessed firsthand. It told him enough. One day he'd hear it all. One day he wouldn't let her deny him any part of her soul....

THIS TIME when Tess entered the courtroom, her parents and Winn were with her. Rae had offered to tend Scotty. Five months into her first pregnancy, she doted on her nephew. If the judge wanted to see Scotty one more time, Rae would drive him downtown.

"You look beautiful, honey. I've never been prouder of you in my life," her dad whispered as they walked down the aisle to the front and sat down, ignoring the already assembled Marsden clan.

"Thank you, Daddy. Oh, I'm so scared."

"Just hold on to me."

"That's all I ever do."

"Don't ever stop." He smiled. "At a time like this, I feel sorry for anyone who doesn't have Alex on their side."

"I've thought that from the first moment we met in his office."

While they'd been talking, Alex had come down the aisle to converse with the court reporter. Tess couldn't help staring at his dark hair and distinctive profile. A slate blue suit she hadn't seen before molded his powerful body.

There were degrees of beauty in both women and men. As far as Tess was concerned, Alex Sommerfield was breathtakingly beautiful. But that was because he was a man of substance and integrity. A rock. Honest till it hurt. A great man by anyone's standards. The greatest by her own.

Perhaps because she'd been concentrating so hard on him he sensed her thoughts. Whatever the reason, he looked over his shoulder and met her gaze. They hadn't seen each other since he'd come to her parents' home. It had seemed like forever. But now he was here.

His silent message said it was going to be all right. She'd make it through her Gethsemane.

At their first meeting, he'd told her she wouldn't lose her son. She'd believed him then. She believed him now.

In the periphery she saw the bailiff take his place. "All rise. The Third District Court of El Paso County, Colorado Springs, Colorado, is now in session, Judge Rutherford T. Larkin presiding. You may be seated."

Leaning on his cane, the judge entered the room and sat down. To Tess, it felt like the pretrial all over again—with one exception. Instead of Clive Medor telling the court how cruel she'd been to his client,

Grant took the witness stand and was sworn in to testify against her.

He'd come to the trial immaculately dressed, appearing at ease. He always looked and smelled good. Those traits had never changed. Unfortunately neither had some others, like his anger...

Medor stepped forward. After the initial questioning, he got down to business. "Mr. Marsden, please tell the court in your own words what life was like living with the defendant."

"I guess from day one I felt like I'd saved up all this money to buy something I wanted at the store, but when I took it home, I wasn't allowed to touch it or play with it. Just look, because it had a defect."

Tess felt her mother's hand reach for hers.

"Are you saying that your wife was not a wife to you in the connubial sense?"

"No. I'm not saying that. She did her duty."

"Then you're saying that her affection was given begrudgingly."

"Yes and no. She was moody."

Tess blinked.

"Did you talk to her about this problem?"

"Yes, but she insisted there wasn't anything wrong. She's very close to her family. Our honeymoon at her parents' cabin in Vail wasn't what I'd hoped it would be because, I figured, she was missing them. She acted depressed. I thought when we got back to our new apartment and she could be around her family, she'd return to normal. But she never did."

"In other words, she continued to be depressed."

"Yes. With a woman like Tessa, it's impossible to have a real conversation. She won't fight. She cries a lot when she thinks I don't know about it. When I try to reach her, she has this way of just looking through me. I know depression can do that to people."

Tess averted her eyes. He was a master at mixing lies with the truth. So much so, he no doubt believed everything he was saying.

"You say she continued to be in this state after the honeymoon."

"Yes. What I started noticing were mood swings, though I didn't call them that at the time. Even around her family she'd get depressed. Sometimes when I suggested she go visit her mom or dad, she'd say no, that she preferred to stay home. Other times she acted so excited I couldn't keep up with her, but she never stayed happy for long. Her parents must have known about her depression, but no one ever bothered to tell me how serious it was."

Tess cringed. Grant sounded so convincing she was terrified Alex would start wondering about her.

"Did you suggest she get help?"

"You don't say things like that to Tessa, and I would never have broached the subject with Dr. Jenner. He's a noted doctor, after all. I was just a college kid from a family who doesn't have any money.

What did I know about anything? Only once did I suggest to him that she might be on something to cope with her depression. He ignored me and told me to leave his house.''

At this point, her dad took Tess's other hand.

"The truth is, after a couple of weeks of being married to her, I realized she was sick. Really sick.''

No, Grant. You're the one who's sick.

"Did you go to anybody for help? A marriage counselor?''

"The pastor who married us does counseling. But I didn't turn to him about Tessa's condition until after Scotty was born and she had a nervous breakdown.''

"If it please the court, Your Honor," said Medor, "I've entered an affidavit signed by Pastor Lowell Carr, testifying to the fact that my client has been a loyal consistent churchgoer who never discussed his marital problems until after she was diagnosed as manic-depressive. And only then did he seek his help as a certified marriage counselor. The pastor also testified that Tessa Marsden and her mother became uncooperative when he tried to counsel her two months ago.''

Tess glanced at her mom and they squeezed hands again.

Medor plunged ahead. "Did you ever consider divorce?''

Grant shook his head. "No. I was her husband. Like a fool, I thought over time I could help her. But that dream died when her psychiatrist diagnosed her as manic-depressive and put her on medication for the rest of her life."

Thank God Alex knows about that other petition for divorce! Tess could have wept with relief, because Clive Medor's question meant *he* didn't know about it.

"Your Honor, I will postpone examination on the medical points in this case until the expert witnesses, Dr. Howard Milhouse, Dr. Robert Haight and Mr. Lew Orton arrive to testify."

Tess felt physically ill. Her gaze switched frantically to Alex whose veiled blue eyes sent her a private signal to hang on.

"Very good, Counselor. You may proceed."

Medor's satisfied smile turned her stomach. "What has she been like since the birth of your son?"

"Because of the medication, she doesn't cry as much. But she functions as if she isn't all there. I don't mean her mind. I'm talking about her emotions. She goes around detached. Kind of zombie-like. All I know is, Scotty has been deprived of a mother who runs on full throttle, so to speak."

"Is that why you want custody of your son?"

"It's one of the reasons."

"Tell us your other reasons."

"She doesn't use good judgment, and I'm afraid that one day she'll put Scotty's life at risk."

"Give us an example of her poor judgment."

"After the holidays, she took him to Hawaii on a week's vacation. The first time she's ever gone far away from me, and what happens? She meets some foreign fellow. When she returns home she's higher than a kite, like someone on drugs. No sooner does she get back then she takes off for her parents' cabin in Vail with her family, jerking Scotty out of school again when he's already behind."

"Your Honor," Medor interjected, "I'm offering in evidence an affidavit signed by Scotty's teacher, Mrs. Janke, attesting to the fact that Scotty's behind in some of his subjects and has become more withdrawn in the classroom over the past year. It also attests to the fact that his mother's illness has apparently prevented her from getting out for parent-teacher conferences."

That's an outright lie! Tess trembled with rage.

The judge nodded and ordered Grant to proceed.

"When I go up to Vail to surprise her with a romantic evening in mind, hoping to rekindle something, she's not even there. When she does get back around eleven, she goes straight to bed, then I see her having seizurelike symptoms about four in the morning, vomiting from a bad trip on drugs, and Dr. Jenner tells me to get out. All this is going on in front of my five-year-old boy.

"Within a week, during which time she moves in with her parents and I'm not allowed to see my son, she serves me with divorce papers, something she'd never discussed with me, something I'd never contemplated because of our religious beliefs.

"Meanwhile a package comes to my home from this foreign guy. He'd enclosed a note. From its contents, I assumed they'd had an affair. Again, all this was going on in front of Scotty."

Medor held up the note. "If I may, Your Honor, I'm entering the note in evidence. It's written in the hand of Mr. Paul Wong and reads: 'In memory of seven wonderful days that brought me more happiness than I have known in years. Devotedly, Paul.'"

Dear God. She'd had no idea what Paul had written. This was one instance when she wouldn't blame anyone for thinking the worst about her and Paul. Still...

"Has your wife made further contact with this man?"

"He left a message on our answering machine for her to call him. Beyond that, I have no idea what arrangements they've made to meet. For that matter, she could be involved with someone else here in town. God knows, she's got the looks to attract any man she wants." He paused. "That's my worry. Scotty is so little and helpless. If he ends up living with her, he'll be neglected while she pursues other relationships. Her lack of good parental care and judgment are scary. I'd never have a moment's peace from worrying."

His voice shook. "I love my son. He's my life. He's made my world bearable under the most difficult circumstances. I've spent every possible moment I could with him when I wasn't at work. I've been involved in his school activities, his church activities."

Tears rolled down Grant's cheeks. "I've provided for him and will continue to provide for him. I have a home, which I'm renting out at the moment. During the interim, I'm staying with my parents who will help me tend Scotty when I can't be there. I'll work with Tessa on visitation. I beg the court to let me have custody."

"Thank you, Mr. Marsden."

The judge inclined his head toward Alex. "Do you wish to cross-examine?"

"Not at this time, Your Honor. First I would like to call my client to the stand."

"Very well. The court calls the defendant, Tessa Marsden, to come forward and be sworn in."

Tess rose to her feet in agony, answering her parents' show of support with another squeeze of their hands. She'd thought Alex was going to ask Grant questions first. Terrified, she walked to the witness stand on jelly legs, took her oath and sat down.

Because of Alex's approval at the pretrial, she wore her hair in the same French twist today. Except for a different wool suit, this one in dark green, she wore the same white blouse. Being the cynosure of every eye, she wanted to feel her most comfortable.

Alex flashed her a secret smile only she could decipher, and breezed her through the preliminaries. Then, "Mrs. Marsden, you've heard the plaintiff's description of your marriage. Is there anything you'd like to change or clarify for the court?"

She took a deep breath. "Basically, since Christmas, my husband and I haven't lived together. Prior to that, we lived six and a half years as husband and wife. But I don't think I ever knew the man my husband could probably be *if* he'd met the right woman. As for my husband knowing me, today he's no closer to that than when we first met. We've been longtime strangers attempting to be friends and lovers. But our marriage never took. It was a mismatch from the beginning and no one's fault.

"I honestly believe that when Grant and I met, we were blinded by physical attraction, caught up in the excitement of getting married—especially when it seemed everyone else at college was getting married. We were just sort of swept along on that tide and rushed into marriage way too fast. We were both in love with love."

Tess glanced down at her clasped hands for a moment, then up. "I believe that Grant saw me as a femme fatale, that I'd had a lot of experience with men before I married him. The truth is, he was only the second man I'd ever even kissed. Because of the way I was raised, my parents' values, the idea of sleeping with a man before marriage was out of the question.

"I was probably one of the most naive brides around. I realize now what a great disappointment I must have been to him. At the time, however, I felt like a failure, and nothing I could do seemed to please him. If I seemed depressed, it was because our marriage was unhappy.

"I hated to admit to anyone we were having problems. I kept going to school, working on my teaching certificate. I asked for a job at church leading the children's choir, because music is one of my loves. Both these activities gave me pleasure. Then I found out I was pregnant and I was ecstatic."

Tess smiled at the memory before going on. "I had the normal morning sickness and was tired a lot, but when our beautiful baby boy was born it was all worth it." Her expression saddened. "After we brought him home from the hospital, I had problems nursing. But I wanted to nurse because I'd heard it gives your baby the best start. When I couldn't do it, I grew so frustrated I felt like more of a failure. That's when the tears started."

She shook her head. "My obstetrician said that I had postpartum depression, that it was temporary. When I told Dad, he said he'd heard of a psychiatrist, Dr. Milhouse, who treated a lot of women with the same thing, so I went to him.

"To my shock, he hospitalized me and told me I had bipolar disorder. He put me on lithium and Valium, and it changed my life. Grant was right. It made me go around feeling like I was wrapped in cotton swabbing all the time. I hated the feeling, but since I had no choice in the matter, there was nothing to do but get on with my life and live with it. So I finished my classes and graduated."

She smiled softly. "Scotty brought the only joy into my life. When my brother, Winn, invited me to take a trip to Hawaii with him, I jumped at the chance to go someplace fun with Scotty and have a good time. As for Grant, I thought my being away would give him much-needed space.

"That's where I met Paul Wong—he was the manager at our hotel. He doesn't believe in Western medicine. He changed my life by suggesting that I get off all medication, that I probably didn't need it."

Tess's voice caught in her throat, and she gave a little cough. "Uh, I wonder if I might have a glass of water?" The bailiff hurried out to comply, and Tess cleared her throat and went on.

"I couldn't stop thinking about what Paul Wong had said. Upon my return from Hawaii, I kept my appointment with Dr. Milhouse. But I didn't tell him about my plan because I didn't want to offend him. But I confided in him that the trip had made me see I couldn't go on with my marriage. I asked him if he had any suggestions on how I might approach Grant about a divorce.

"He told me to say nothing to Grant until he'd talked with him. Then he made me another appointment and I left. But instead of getting more medication, I went straight to my father's office and told him what I intended to do."

A glass of water was placed before her and she took a sip. With Alex nodding encouragingly, Tess went on to describe her withdrawal, Grant's visit to the cabin, his accusations, his fury at being asked to leave. "He may not have said the words, but he knew just as I did that it was the end of our marriage. That's when I went home and found an attorney, because I didn't want the pain to go on."

She lifted her chin and said firmly, "I will say this. Grant has been a good caring father and Scotty loves him. I never want that to change for either of them, and if I'm granted custody, I'll do everything in my power to ensure that they have the best-possible father-son relationship."

"Mrs. Marsden," Alex said, "would you please tell the court your present circumstances?"

"Scotty and I are now living in our own apartment. Just three days ago I signed a contract with the board of education to be a full-time choral teacher at Liberty High School this fall with a starting salary of $24,000.

"Until school starts, I'm working as teacher's aide at the same high school and will continue to work there this summer."

Her voice wobbled precariously. "I—I can't imagine not being able to nurture and care for my son as I've been doing every day since he was born."

A glow of satisfaction lit Alex's eyes. "Thank you, Mrs. Marsden."

"Counsel for the plaintiff? Do you wish to cross-examine?"

"Not at this time, Your Honor."

"Counselor?" The judge indicated it was Alex's turn.

"I'd like to recall the plaintiff to the stand."

"Mrs. Marsden, you may step down."

Tess obeyed the judge and found her seat between her parents while Grant took the stand.

"You've already been sworn in, Mr. Marsden. You're still under oath."

Grant nodded. Tess's eyes clung to Alex.

"Mr. Marsden, you testified that you never considered divorce an alternative."

"That's right."

"Then would you be willing to explain to the court this document? Your Honor, I have in my hand a copy of a complaint for divorce filed by the plaintiff only three months into their marriage."

"Objection!" Medor was on his feet.

"The court will view the evidence," intoned the judge. "You may both approach the bench."

Alex took the copy to the rostrum for the judge's perusal. Tess could tell by the look Medor sent Grant that he was outraged.

"Objection overruled," pronounced Judge Larkin. "Answer the question, Mr. Marsden."

"I forgot about that petition until just now," Grant said in a quiet voice. "My best friend suggested I get out of my marriage as soon as possible. But I couldn't go through with it."

"Do you remember the grounds for divorce, Mr. Marsden?" When Grant hesitated, he said, "If you don't remember, I'll be glad to help you."

"Not the exact wording," Grant said.

Alex cocked his head. "You filed on the grounds of incompatibility. Nothing was said about your wife's sickness. No mention of her being depressed, unable to cope, crying jags, mood swings. May I suggest that the reason you filed was because you, like your wife, simply realized your marriage wasn't working, which is the reason most people divorce."

"Objection! Counsel is leading the plaintiff."

"Sustained."

"Did you ever tell your wife that you had filed a divorce complaint, but that you'd never had it served?"

Tess could feel Grant's frustration.

"No."

"When she told you at the cabin that she'd never taken cocaine or amphetamines, why didn't you believe her?"

"Because I could tell she was having a bad trip."

"How could you tell?"

"Because I've seen people on drugs."

"She told you it was food poisoning. Mightn't she have been telling the truth? The symptoms are the same."

"I suppose."

"But you assumed she was on drugs. Why would you do that when you knew she was forced to take other medication, anyway?"

"Because Dr.—"

"Objection!" Medor shouted. "This line of questioning is irrelevant, because the court knows the defendant lied to her husband. She told him it was food poisoning when in reality she was having drug withdrawal."

"Overruled, Counselor. Go on, Mr. Marsden."

Alex stood with his legs apart. "Let me help you remember. You said, 'Because Dr.—'"

Grant's head was bowed. "Because her doctor suggested she might be taking illegal drugs."

"Which doctor?"

"Dr. Milhouse, her psychiatrist."

"*He* suggested she might be taking cocaine or amphetamines?"

"Yes."

"So the idea of these drugs didn't originate with you."

"No."

"When did he suggest this?"

"After Tessa got back from Hawaii. She was higher than a kite."

"Wouldn't you be higher than a kite if you thought you might not be manic-depressive, after all, that you might be able to get off all medication and live a normal life?"

"Objection! Counselor is making useless conjecture."

"Sustained. Confine your comments to the relevant points, Counselor."

"Yes, Your Honor. I have no further questions of this witness."

"You may step down, Mr. Marsden. Counsel for the plaintiff, call your first witness."

Medor, looking harassed, jerked his head around to the back of the room. "Has Dr. Robert Haight arrived?"

"I'm here."

With a sense of dread Tess watched the court-appointed psychiatrist take the oath and sit down on the witness stand.

"What is it with these henchmen?" Winn whispered in her hearing. "They've all got beards."

Tess had wondered the same thing. She managed a small smile.

Medor asked the doctor to render his findings to the court.

"My evaluation of Mrs. Marsden is that I found no evidence of bipolar disorder."

"Thank God," her parents both murmured at the same time as Tess said it in her heart.

Medor fumed. "I have no more questions of this witness."

The judge nodded to Alex.

"None, Your Honor."

"Then call your next witness, Counselor."

Medor turned around again and beckoned Lew Orton to the stand.

CHAPTER FIFTEEN

"It's almost over, honey," her father whispered.

"I know."

"Mr. Orton, please tell the court your findings."

"I've worked with the Marsden family for five weeks, and in my opinion, both parents have problems that have contributed to the son's insecurity. However, the father is the healthier of the two and the more giving parent. It is my recommendation that he be granted immediate custody of the boy."

Medor broke out in his Cheshire-cat grin. "I have no further questions of this witness."

When the judge turned to Alex, he got to his feet. "I have several." He looked at the witness.

"Mr. Orton, after her last group-therapy session with you, you called my client in for a conference. Would you tell the court what you told her?"

"I suggested she needed more therapy sessions."

"Why?"

"Because she fights authority and evades questions she doesn't want to answer. It's a form of intimidation that has a derogatory effect on children."

"What else did you tell her?"

"Nothing else."

"You didn't tell her you were going to put her on more medication to control her?"

"I'm not a medical doctor and couldn't prescribe for her."

"I'll rephrase. Did you tell her you might have to get her put on medication?"

"Well, I might have indicated something along those lines to let her know how serious this was."

"Is intimidation your normal practice?"

"Objection!"

"Overruled. Answer the question, Mr. Orton."

He rubbed his beard. "When Mrs. Marsden walks in a room, it's like a volcano going off. Everyone stops. Everyone looks. She has learned she can manipulate people. She's unteachable."

"Is that why you told your therapy group to beat up on her, verbally speaking?"

"Objection, Your Honor. Counsel is questioning the integrity of an expert witness of the court."

Alex walked over to the bench. "I have here a signed affidavit from one of the patients in the therapy group attesting to the fact that Mr. Orton told the group to 'rough her up.' Those are his exact words."

Even from the distance, Tessa could see the judge looking askance at Lew Orton. "Objection overruled."

"No more questions, Your Honor."

You may step down, Mr. Orton.'' The judge looked at Medor. ''Counselor, call your last witness.''

''It's Dr. Howard Milhouse, Your Honor. He should be out in the hall.''

This was Clive Medor's triumphant moment. Tess shivered. Even if Dr. Milhouse had been called up on charges, nothing had been proved. In the American judicial system, you were innocent until proved guilty. Therefore his testimony would stand.

Tess's mother put her arm around her shoulders. ''It's going to be all right, darling.''

''I don't know, Mom. I'm terrified.'' She glanced at Alex. For once he didn't respond. His jaw had hardened, giving him a faintly glacial look. He'd fought so hard and long for her. If he lost the case, Tessa would suffer for the rest of her life. Not only for the loss of her son, but for Alex's loss. *Dear Father in heaven. Help me. Help him. Help all of us.*

The hushed murmur of voices in the courtroom made her turn her head. ''Is he coming?''

''I don't see him,'' her father said.

''Is he here, Counselor?''

''Any second, Your Honor.''

''The court doesn't have time to wait, Mr. Medor. It's past lunchtime now. I have Dr. Milhouse's remarks in evidence and wish to bring this case to a close. If there are no more witnesses to come forth, you may make your final remarks.''

''But Your Honor, he's—''

"Careful, Counselor, or I'll find you in contempt. Make your summation now."

Medor flung himself out of his seat. "The evidence presented in this case speaks for itself. Counseling Services has recommended that my client be given immediate custody of the boy. His wife's psychiatrist of four years' standing has treated her for manic-depression and has testified that her illness puts her son, Scotty, at great risk. To award custody of the boy to the mother would be a contravention of his best interests. Therefore, my client wishes to retain custody of his son."

"I feel like I'm going to die," Tess whispered to her mother.

"No, you're not, honey. Let's listen to Alex."

"Your Honor, this is a straightforward divorce case. There is no evidence to support the fact that the child, Scotty, has been damaged by the mother. He may be behind in a couple of subjects in school. So is every child who takes a vacation. And in America these days, children vacation with their parents any time the parent can get away.

"Mr. Orton has testified that the parents' deficiencies have contributed to the child's insecurity. Show me a child who isn't insecure when the parents are considering a permanent separation."

He paused, as if to let the court digest this, then resumed. "Dr. Haight has testified that my client shows no signs of bipolar disorder. Testimony from a signed affidavit, which I will enter as final evidence, comes from her obstetrician, temporarily residing in South Africa.''

He unfolded the document in his hand. ''Dr. Williams states, 'Never at any time did I witness my patient in a state of depression. Only when her frustration over not being able to nurse was further enhanced by the hormonal changes in her body, did I suggest that she was suffering from postpartum depression. I told her it would probably go away within six weeks, but if it continued, to consult a doctor who knew more about such things.'''

Alex handed the document to the judge, then began to list the facts. ''The plaintiff intended to divorce my client three months into their marriage on the grounds of incompatibility, nothing else.

''The affidavits in the pretrial hearing from the hospital in Vail attest to my client's hospitalization for the express purpose of monitoring her heart during drug withdrawal.

''The plaintiff has never once said that his wife was not a good mother. The mother has been home with the child from the day he was born. Both the plaintiff and defendant have testified that they haven't gone on any trips to speak of.

''The defendant is drug free and intends to stay that way for the rest of her life. She has been forced to sustain abuse by a court-appointed social worker who frightened her by telling her she had to go back on drugs.''

Alex paused for a breath. With a glance at Medor, he went on, ''The only witness who has seen my client on a regular long-term basis, Dr. Howard Milhouse, is not available for testimony. I believe, Your Honor, that is because he is up on charges of malpractice and won't be appearing in this court or any other for some time to come.''

There was a collective gasp in the courtroom. ''I have it on good authority from his mother, Mrs. Lucille Milhouse, who was committed to a sanatorium by Dr. Milhouse on his own say-so,'' Alex continued, ''that he has left the state of Colorado, and not even she knows where he is.

''Forty-four women like my client have been going to him for bipolar disorder. As it turns out, none of them may have the disorder. We know one woman who doesn't. She's sitting in this courtroom today.''

He paused again and nodded in Tessa's direction. ''Despite four years of unquestionable hell due to a misdiagnosis, my client has raised a wonderful son and has survived impossible odds including gossip, innuendo and bias, even from loved ones and close friends who didn't know the truth.

''She's a God-fearing, intelligent, beautiful, healthy, well-rounded woman with a teaching career ahead of her. She wishes to retain custody of her son and will do everything in her power to make certain her son and husband enjoy as much time together as possible. To date she has complied fully with visitation, in fact, has bent over backwards to make it a pleasant experience for Scotty.

"He's a charming, delightful little fellow who will lose much of his insecurity when this case is brought to a close and everyone can get on with their lives. Thank you."

Winn and her father both let loose a whispered but fervent "Yes!" Tess feared the judge heard them, but he didn't remark on it. He simply took off his glasses and said, "I don't know about you, but I'm hungry. Having gathered all the facts, I'll take them under advisement. Counsel for the plaintiff and the defendant will be apprised of my written decision when I hand it down at a later date.

"Until such time, the defendant will continue to retain temporary custody of the boy. Off the record, he *is* a charming boy. This court is adjourned." He pounded his gavel and left the courtroom.

The trial was over.

Tess sat there, stunned, trying to take in that she still had custody of Scotty.

Her family swarmed around Alex, her father and brother slapping him on the back, her mother hugging him, weeping unashamedly. *They love him, too,* Tess thought.

Light-headed from the trauma, Tess tried to get up and had to sit down again. Suddenly Alex was at her side with a glass of water. She drained it, then looked into his eyes.

"Thank you, Alex. That's all I ever say to you. It's so inadequate after what you've done for me. Whatever decision the judge renders, I'll never forget how you championed me."

"It was my privilege, Tess." His voice seemed to resonate through her being. "Until that decision comes, remember that the judge was speaking to you and you alone when he said you had a charming son. Keep that in mind."

She nodded. "You said his decision might be a long time in coming. I'm resigned to it, and so thankful to be able to keep Scotty with me until then I'm not going to complain."

The awareness between them crackled like a live wire. "You're a rare breed of woman, Tessa Marsden. I feel honored to have known you."

He's saying goodbye. Dear God! The emptiness. It's too much!

"I—I'm the one who's honored. Only a magnificent human being could have done what you did today. There's no one like you. So...good luck." She forced herself to say it, to let him go.

His features sobered. "I'll let you know the second I learn of the decision."

She nodded.

"I'm late for a conference with a client."

"Then hurry. I know what it's like to need you, Counselor. Don't keep them waiting any longer than necessary."

She watched his long strides carry him from the courtroom—and felt herself die a little.

"OH, RAE. Amy's so beautiful! I know you two have had a long wait for your first child, but she's worth it!" The perfect little features and rosebud mouth tugged at Tess's heart.

"That's because she takes after you and Winn."

Tess shook her head. "She has your skin and blond hair. Scotty was born bald. As I was bearing down for the last time, my doctor said, 'My, your baby has such a nice shiny head.' I was so positive my child would be born with a lot of hair like Amy, I told him it couldn't possibly be mine. Everyone in the delivery room roared."

Rae burst into laughter, too, then kissed the top of her little girl's head. "Scotty's certainly made up for it with all that natural curl. I think he's going to be tall like Winn."

"Scotty loves it that he's the second-tallest boy in his first-grade class. But you never know. Grant's five foot eleven. If Scotty's as tall as his dad, that'll make him happy."

"Does he like his new teacher?"

"He adores her. She has a sunny disposition, the total opposite of Mrs. Janke."

"How's school going for you?"

"Good. There's a nice blend of voices this year and a handful of students with real talent. I'm thinking of putting on an operetta right after Thanksgiving."

"Which one?"

"*The Song of Norway.*"

"Grieg. I love his music."

"Me, too."

"That's ambitious. After-school rehearsals. Evening practices."

"That's what I need. Lots of work."

"You need to start dating."

Tess shook her head. "I'm still a married woman, Rae."

"Oh, for heaven's sake. I've heard Grant is seeing someone else. The trial was over ages ago!"

Tess knew exactly how long it had been. Five months almost to the day since she and Alex had said goodbye to each other in that courtroom. Not a word or a phone call from him since. It was as if he'd disappeared off the face of the planet. And the divorce still hadn't been granted.

"I won't do anything that would jeopardize keeping Scotty."

It was Friday evening. Grant's weekend for visitation. She'd kissed her son goodbye just before coming over to the hospital to see Rae and Amy.

Fridays without Scotty were the worst. She always felt at a loose end. That was when she had too much time to think, and thinking was the one thing she'd learned never to do if she wanted to survive. Maybe she'd take a drive into the mountains after she left the hospital.

"Grant doesn't know what you do."

"Oh, yes, he does." Her voice shook. "Scotty is his innocent informant. One wrong move and he'll call the judge."

"That's horrible."

"Now that you have a baby, you're going to find out that your life is an open book because a child notices all, tells all, without even thinking about it."

"Grant has no right to keep tabs on you."

"It's a habit, Rae. Yesterday I got a note from his mother. She said she was trying to forgive me for ruining her son's life."

"Oh, brother. I hope you burned it."

"Actually I did."

"Good for you. Honestly, Tess—" she sighed "—I don't know how you've stood any of it. Winn's nicknamed you Superwoman."

"I wish I had some of her powers. I'd lasso Scotty and we'd take a giant leap to Hawaii, away from the long arm of the law."

"Mmm..." Rae made a sleepy sound. "We'd be right behind you."

Rae looked very happy and very tired. The pain-killer the nurse had given her was taking effect. Tess kissed her sister-in-law's forehead, then leaned over the sleeping infant and put her in the crib next to the bed.

Looking at the two of them brought back the joyful memory of the morning Scotty was born. But everything else was a nightmare, an ongoing nightmare, because now she was living on borrowed time. Any day, any week, any month now, Scotty could be taken from her. Most of the time she refused to let herself dwell on it.

Wheeling around, she left the hospital and got into her car. Without conscious thought she turned onto the freeway.

It was a mistake. She found herself in the middle of five-o'clock rush-hour traffic. It would take at least forty-five minutes to get across town for that drive into the mountains.

Fifteen minutes later, however, a compulsion she couldn't resist caused her to exit the turnoff that led to the Crane building. As if she were on automatic pilot, she found herself pulling into a parking space near the entrance.

Her talk with Rae had done its damage.

She sat there for a while, avidly watching for the one face that haunted her every living moment. Then it occurred to her that he probably parked in the un-

derground lot and wouldn't be walking out the front
doors.

Her gaze flicked to the sixth floor. He might still be
there. And if he was, would he be annoyed that she'd
come to see him when she had no legitimate reason?
Did she dare bother him when she knew this was the
time of day he returned phone calls to frantic clients
who needed his assurance so they could make it
through another night? How many of those had he
made to her?

Would he be glad to see her? Had he missed her at
all?

Every question of self-doubt tortured her until she
thought she'd go crazy. But this was the closest she'd
been to him in months, and she couldn't bring herself to drive away.

Finally, when she knew she couldn't bear it a second longer, she got out of the car and hurried into the
building.

Dry-mouthed, she waited for people to exit the elevator, then rode alone to his floor. It was as empty
as a tomb. With a sinking sensation, she approached
the doors of his suite. After another internal battle,
she quietly turned the knob, but it didn't give.

She groaned in disappointment and started to move
away when it dawned on her that, though his paralegal and clerks may have gone for the night, he could
still be in there working.

She summoned up her courage and knocked on the heavy oak door several times. Then she waited.

When there was no response, she could have cried aloud her frustration. She rapped again, but it was apparent no one was inside. For all she knew he was out of the city, maybe even the country, be it for business or pleasure.

She should never have come. It only made her heartache that much more acute.

It wasn't until she pushed the button to summon the elevator that she heard someone call her name. She turned in the direction of the low masculine voice and saw a man's powerful frame filling the aperture of a door a few feet down from the main office entrance.

"Lord. It *is* you!"

"Alex," she whispered in shock, and moved toward him.

He looked good. So incredibly good. The same way he'd looked on that icy night months ago when she'd come to his office. No jacket or tie. Just his shirtsleeves.

She rubbed moist palms against her hips, wishing she'd put on something beautiful, instead of showing up in the simple denim dress she'd worn to school. Her hair was still in a ponytail.

"I—I know you don't have any news for me yet," she said hesitantly. "To be honest, I'm not sure why I came. Now I feel like a fool."

His eyes narrowed on her mouth. "I've driven by your apartment more times than I care to admit, hoping to catch a glimpse of you."

A soft gasp escaped. "Why didn't you stop and come in?"

"You *know* why," he said hoarsely.

She averted her eyes. "You mean b-because of Scotty."

To her surprise, he pulled her through the doorway and into a storeroom-cum-kitchen, then shut the door and wedged her against a refrigerator.

"I mean because of this," and his dark head descended, his mouth covering hers hungrily.

Tess clung to him, kissing him back with equal passion, a passion that had been building ever since she'd first set eyes on him.

"Tess..." he moaned, kissing every inch of her face and throat, "I've wanted you for too long. I knew this would happen if we were ever alone together."

She pressed closer, until it seemed their bodies were molded to each other. "I couldn't stay away another minute," she confessed against his mouth before it devoured hers again, obliterating coherent thought.

It could have been a lifetime later when he said, "Help me to stop."

"I can't. I don't ever want to let you go. Please...just a few more minutes." Her desire for him was like a raging fever. Delirious with longing, she sought his mouth again.

"Tess—" his voice sounded slurred "—you have no idea what you're doing to me. I'm warning you—" his fingers bit into her shoulders "—I've reached the point where you're the one who's going to have to pull away from me."

She knew that if she did pull away from him, he wouldn't reach for her again. He was too honorable. As soon as she left his arms, her life would be a desert once more, with no guarantees how long she'd have to wait before her marriage was dissolved. Though she'd removed her rings, legally, and in God's eyes, she was still Mrs. Marsden.

Summoning every vestige of willpower, she broke another one of his soul-destroying kisses and stepped away, her chest heaving.

On a moan of protest, he reached out and caught her hand. His eyes glazed, his breathing shallow, he said, "Don't come to the office again, or I won't be responsible for my actions."

She swallowed hard. "I—I'll stay away."

"Lord . . . don't look at me like that!"

She trembled. "I'm sorry."

"Tess, Medor senses there's something going on between you and me."

She nodded. "Grant's already accused me of the same thing." She sighed. "It's ironic when you consider that he's seeing another woman."

With a reluctance she could feel, Alex let go of her hand. "No matter what your husband does, you and I have to avoid even the least appearance of anything personal between us. You need to understand that the judge isn't keeping you in suspense because he's a sadist.

"He's purposely letting time go by to see how life unfolds day after day before he hands down his verdict. He wants to see if visitation runs smoothly, if your depression has truly gone for good. If it hasn't, then he wants to know how you'll handle it, how stable you really are."

"I realize that," said Tessa, "but it's so hard!"

Alex nodded. "I know. The judge is watching both parents to see how you conduct your lives. Scotty is his one concern. It's a wise judge who takes a long time making this kind of a decision. There's less chance of the Supreme Court overturning his decision when so much time and thought have been put into it."

She gasped. "If Grant loses, you think he'll appeal it?"

"My gut instinct says no. I believe your husband's motivation for trying to get custody of Scotty was based on a desire to hurt you for cheating him out of his happiness, rather than on a consuming need to raise his son. By the time the judge hands down his ruling, your husband will probably have lost interest in the case."

His eyes looked bleak, revealing the same kind of emptiness she was feeling. "The months have been dragging by. Your husband has already started to crack under the strain. Time will invariably decide the right person to be Scotty's custodial parent. I'd wager my life on the judge choosing you...and so I won't do anything that could jeopardize that decision.''

He meant he wouldn't see her. His unselfishness gave ultimate proof that he was the prince among men she'd always seen him as. She'd never loved him more than at this moment.

Struggling for breath, she said, "The wait is tearing me apart, but I understand." After a slight hesitation, "I...if these few minutes are all I can ever have of you, then I thank God for that much.''

Not lingering to hear his response, she flew out the door and dashed down the stairs at the end of the hall. She couldn't afford to wait for the elevator. If she didn't get away from him quickly, she was afraid she wouldn't leave at all.

When she was back in her car, she sat there for a long time, attempting to get a hold on her emotions, but a new fear plagued her.

By the time the judge finally made his ruling, anything might have happened. Alex could have met another woman, even married her. The possibility devastated her, but it was a bitter reality she had to face.

Thank heaven she had Scotty. He was her life. Nevertheless, she wouldn't give up hope that one day Alex Sommerfield would be an integral part of it. Until then, she'd concentrate on her son and his happiness.

CHAPTER SIXTEEN

THERE WAS NO BLUER sky in the world than a Colorado sky on a sunny June day. The whole world looked reborn, but Alex felt no particular joy as his car ate up the miles to Colorado Springs from Pueblo, where he'd taken a deposition in a new case.

Thank God it was Friday afternoon. He would return to the office and deal with last-minute business, then grab his sleeping bag and head on over to the house. Now that the roof was on, he could spend the weekend there.

Winn Marsden was not only a great architect, he'd become a close friend. Tess's brother was the only reason Alex was still functioning. He couldn't have survived this enforced celibacy otherwise.

Nine long months had gone by since she'd come late to his office and lit a fire in him that threatened to burn him alive. Two months ago, he'd argued another case before Judge Larkin. It had taken great strength of will not to ask him when he intended to make his ruling in the Marsden case.

Alex had told Tess there were perfectly good reasons she had to be patient with this judge. To Alex's chagrin, he was finding it impossible to live with his own advice. The temptation to go to her had him on the verge of turning over his cases to his new partner and leaving the country till the case was settled. He was that close to ruining everything in his desperation to be with the woman who'd transformed his life.

An hour later he was on the elevator to the sixth floor. As he let himself in the back way, he heard, "Boss!"

Alex frowned. "Burt? I told you to take off early today. What are you still doing here?"

His paralegal appeared in the kitchen waving an envelope. "This was just hand-delivered from Judge Larkin's chambers."

Alex stopped dead in his tracks.

TESS PEEKED through the curtain as Grant drove away with Scotty for the weekend. It was always hard to see her son leave, particularly since today had been the last day of school for both of them.

Dreading to be alone tonight of all nights, she'd made tentative arrangements to go to a nightclub with some of the faculty to celebrate, but her heart wasn't in it.

When the phone rang, she answered, assuming it was one of them making last-minute arrangements. But to her surprise, the caller was Winn. Just hearing his voice made her happy.

"Tessie, Rae told me this is Grant's weekend for visitation. Since Amy has a cold and I have to drive out to Spruce Lake to meet with the owner of a house I've designed, how about coming with me?"

"Those lucky people," she mused aloud. Spruce Lake was a wooded area recently developed and zoned for residences. In Tess's opinion, it was the most beautiful spot in Colorado Springs.

"Does that mean you'll come?"

She chuckled. "I'd half planned to spend the evening with some teachers, but I'd much rather drive out there with you and see your latest masterpiece. How soon do you want to leave?"

"Right now. I'll be there in ten minutes."

"That sounds wonderful. Thanks for thinking of me. Did I ever tell you you're the best brother on earth?"

"All the time, but I never get tired of hearing it. Hurry and get ready. Wear something warm. The evenings are still chilly."

As soon as they hung up, Tess phoned one of her colleagues and told her she'd had a change in plans. Then she dashed into the bedroom to find a pair of jeans and a sweatshirt.

She'd always loved going to building sites with Winn. Until her tragic marriage, she'd lived for the day when the beautiful lake house Winn had once designed for her became a reality.

A half hour later, she let out a cry of stunned surprise when they wound through the trees bordering the lake and came upon the very dwelling that formed part of the fabric of her dashed dreams.

"My house!"

"That's right," he said with a half smile.

Winn had never been cruel to her in his life, but he could have no idea of the pain he'd just inflicted.

"Don't you like it, Tessie?"

"Of course I like it." Her voice came out more like a croak. He sounded so happy she couldn't let him know of the deep wound he'd inflicted.

"Go ahead and take a look inside while I wait here for the owner. You can get in through those sliding doors leading into the living room."

Winn really wanted her to inspect the house. With a sinking heart, she got out of the car and walked slowly toward it. Though the sun wouldn't fall below the horizon for a while yet, the pines cast long shadows across the rock-and-wood exterior.

The two-story house with its sundeck and picture windows captured the rustic look of the West, yet possessed a modern feel and blended into the wooded landscape as if it had grown there. The unmistakable stamp of her brother's genius appeared in every detail of the design.

She opened the glass doors and stepped inside— and for a moment the earth stood still. Someone was standing near the fireplace at one end of the living room, a slow smile transforming his handsome features.

Alex. It was Alex.

Suddenly she was running toward him, and then there was no space between them at all. Arms, legs, bodies entwined. Mouths fused in unleashed passion all the more consuming because they could finally give vent to their emotions.

He cried her name in joy. She heard the love, felt his tears mingling with her own. Then those lips for which she'd hungered for so long began devouring hers again with a passion that left her breathless.

She couldn't talk, couldn't think. There was only this moment, this prince of men in her arms, loving her, needing her....

Neither of them heard the footsteps.

"Welcome to the family, Alex," a familiar voice said in the near darkness. Tess and Alex pulled slightly apart and looked over. "My sister's been waiting a lifetime for you."

"Winn!" She burrowed her face into Alex's shoulder in acute embarrassment. He crushed her against him possessively.

Winn chuckled. "Obviously you forgot I was outside waiting, but no one deserves their privacy more than the two of you. I'm going home to give Mom and Dad the good news."

When he pulled the door closed, Alex cupped Tess's hot face in his hands. His eyes worshiped her, as he said, "Your brother knows exactly how I feel about you, how I've always felt about you. At exactly five-twenty this afternoon, I found out you were a free woman who'd been given permanent custody of her son. I came to claim you—if you'll have me." His voice trembled. "I'm in love with you, Tess. I have been since the first day."

"I'm in love with *you,*" she said against his mouth. "I knew something monumental had happened to me the second you took my hand when we first met. You told me then I wouldn't lose my son. I've loved you from that moment on."

"Tess—"

"It's true, my darling. Nine empty months without being able to tell you how I feel, to show you...it's been torture beyond enduring. To think it's finally over, that you're here in my arms. That you love me. You love *me.*"

"Yes...so much, I want to marry you tonight. But I know that's asking the impossible."

She looked up at him. "Why?"

His throat worked convulsively. "Scotty's going to need time to get used to me. To us."

"What if I told you he knows I'm in love with you?" She chuckled. "It's our little secret. He thinks you'd make a 'cool' stepfather."

"You're serious..."

"Yes, my love."

Alex crushed her in his arms once more. "I know a judge who'll marry us whenever we say."

"Can we fly to Hawaii right after?"

"I'm way ahead of you."

"Now *I'm* asking the impossible. You can't just walk away from your law practice on a moment's notice."

"Oh, yes, I can. During the time you and I have been apart, I've taken a partner."

"That's wonderful!" she cried. "You've needed someone to share the load. You work way too hard."

He rubbed his hands up and down her arms. "I did it with us in mind, Tess. We're going to be a family, and we're going to turn this house into a home. I crave a life with you, Tess. I want to have children with you."

"I do, too," she breathed. "I do, too."

His eyes smoldered. "I plan to be there for you all the way. Too much time has been wasted as it is."

"Oh, I agree." She threw her arms around his neck. "Our life together can't begin soon enough."

"We'll take Scotty to Hawaii with us."

"I love you for saying that, but I'd like to have my new husband to myself. I'm sure Grant will be glad to keep Scotty while we're away. The visitations have been going well, and Grant actually seems happier than I've ever seen him."

She paused, then said, a smile lighting her face, "On Sunday night, when Scotty comes home, we'll tell him our news together. He already likes you, Alex. It won't be long before he loves you. It'll be a different kind of love than he has for his father, but love all the same."

"My darling," Alex murmured into her hair, "I wish my grandparents could have met you—they raised me after my parents were killed. They would have loved you."

"Well, my parents adore you. So does Winn. Oh, Alex . . . I want to know everything about you."

"You will, but all you need to know is that I've fallen hopelessly in love with you and want to spend the rest of my life with you."

With that heartfelt declaration, Alex lowered his head and kissed her long and hard.

Minutes later, breathless and so filled with joy she thought she'd burst, Tess whispered feverishly, "I can't wait to thank Paul Wong. If it hadn't been for him, I would never have met you. I don't even want to think what would've happened if Roger Thorn hadn't recommended you. Or worse . . . if you had turned down my case."

"No more thinking, Tess," Alex said, his eyes soft with feeling. "No more what-ifs. We've defied all the odds. Now it's our turn to live. Our turn to love."

BRIDE'S BAY RESORT

UNLOCK THE DOOR TO GREAT ROMANCE AT BRIDE'S BAY RESORT

Join Harlequin's new across-the-lines series, set in an exclusive hotel on an island off the coast of South Carolina.

Seven of your favorite authors will bring you exciting stories about fascinating heroes and heroines discovering love at Bride's Bay Resort.

Look for these fabulous stories coming to a store near you beginning in January 1996.

Harlequin American Romance #613 in January
Matchmaking Baby by Cathy Gillen Thacker

Harlequin Presents #1794 in February
Indiscretions by Robyn Donald

Harlequin Intrigue #362 in March
Love and Lies by Dawn Stewardson

Harlequin Romance #3404 in April
Make Believe Engagement by Day Leclaire

Harlequin Temptation #588 in May
Stranger in the Night by Roseanne Williams

Harlequin Superromance #695 in June
Married to a Stranger by Connie Bennett

Harlequin Historicals #324 in July
Dulcie's Gift by Ruth Langan

Visit Bride's Bay Resort each month wherever Harlequin books are sold.

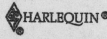

HARLEQUIN®

BBAYG

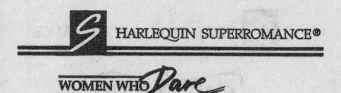

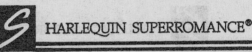

HARLEQUIN SUPERROMANCE®

SHOWCASE

Do you want to fall in love with a purrfect hero?
To be purrfectly entertained by a purrfectly wonderful
romance? (Or do you just love cats?)

Then don't miss

YOU AGAIN

by

Peggy Nicholson

"Tantalizing and seductively unique. Don't miss
You Again. It's purrrfect!"
—Dee Holmes, author of *His Runaway Son*

"*You Again* is delectable, delightfully different... In a
word, magnificat!"
—Anne McAllister, author of the Code of the West trilogy

"A wonderfully original, thoroughly enchanting tale that is
sure to please lovers of romance and cats alike."
—Antoinette Stockenberg, author of *Emily's Ghost*

"Suspenseful, frequently humorous, and always engaging,
You Again is impossible to put down until the final,
wonderfully satisfying page is turned."
—Kay Hooper, author of *Amanda*

HARLEQUIN SUPERROMANCE®

If you've always felt there's something special about a
man raising a family on his own...
You won't want to miss Harlequin Superromance's
touching series

FAMILY
MAN

He's sexy, he's single...and he's a father!
Can any woman resist?

HIS RUNAWAY SON
by Dee Holmes

Detective Burke Wheeler's son is in trouble.
Now he's run away, and Burke and his ex-wife,
Abby, have to work together to find him. Join the
search in this exciting, emotional love story.
Available in July.

Be sure to watch for upcoming FAMILY MAN titles.
Fall in love with our sexy fathers, each determined to do
the best he can for his kids.

Look for them wherever Harlequin books are sold.

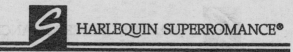

HARLEQUIN SUPERROMANCE®

Come West with us!

In Superromance's series of Western romances you can
visit a ranch—and fall in love with a rancher!

In July watch for

She Caught the Sheriff
by Anne Marie Duquette

**Let us take you to the Silver Dollar Ranch,
near Tombstone, Arizona.**

Rancher Wyatt Bodine is also the town sheriff. But
he's never had a case like this before! Someone's left
a hundred-year-old skeleton in Boot Hill Cemetery—
practically at the feet of visiting forensic investigator
Caro Hartlan. Needless to say, Caro offers to help the
handsome sheriff find out "who done it"—and why!

Look for upcoming HOME ON THE RANCH
titles wherever Harlequin books are sold.

Bestselling authors

ELAINE COFFMAN
RUTH LANGAN

and

MARY McBRIDE

Together in one fabulous collection!

OUTLAW Brides

Available in June wherever Harlequin
books are sold.

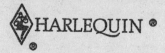

HARLEQUIN ®